UNDER A
MARTIAN
SKY

ANTHONY
FUCILLA

Published 2023 by arima publishing

www.arimapublishing.com

ISBN 978 1 84549 818 4

© Anthony Fucilla 2023

Swirl is an imprint of arima publishing.

arima publishing
ASK House, Northgate Avenue
Bury St Edmunds, Suffolk IP32 6BB
t: (+44) 01284 717884

www.arimapublishing.com

OTHER BOOKS BY THE AUTHOR:

Novellas

THE MARS TIME-PROJECT

BEYOND EARTH'S HORIZON

Short Story Collections

QUANTUM CHRONICLES
IN THE ELEVENTH DIMENSION

QUANTUM CHRONICLES 2

IMPERIAL PLANET

SILENT EARTH

ANDROIDS AND THE GODS

THE GOLDEN MOONS OF JUPITER

Cover Design: Gary Pope - studio@pjpdesign.com

UNDER A MARTIAN SKY:

ANTHONY FUCILLA

UNDER A MARTIAN SKY

Chapter 1 – In the Beginning

THE NEXT colossal step in Man's evolution was the conquest of MARS. That universal dominant force, Mankind, had finally reached the mysterious Red Planet and colonised it. That speck of matter, a vast collection of atoms with constant albedo changes which ancient eyes had studied from afar since the beginning of time was now home to that mysterious creature, Man. A cosmic explosion, the Big Bang, the father of all life, however triggered, was responsible for the formation of the Red Planet as well as space and time itself, that inescapable electromagnetic field.

As Mankind reckoned it, Mars formed 4.5 billion years ago inside a solar nebula where dust particles clumped together to form a planet. Eventually an entire system of planets formed with the Sun sitting merrily in the centre twisting and turning in the magnetic fields of its own creation. But within the solar-system, Mars and the blue planet Earth had a special affinity. They were sisters, born together in the seething maelstrom of dust and gas, each world going through a period of chaotic violence as monstrous rocks rained down crashing violently and unforgivingly into each world in a holocaust of devilish explosions, the monstrous rocks themselves liquefying into bubbling magma as they hit the surface. As a result of the fiery chaos, there could be no solid ground. Each of these explosions released heat that melted surrounding rock and the Sun's radiance, emanating from that giant nuclear reactor, could not penetrate either world as steaming clouds engulfed each planet. Slowly each world coalesced as a result of gravity. Through the course of time, solid land formed via hydrostatic equilibrium. However, Mars was dwarfed by its neighbour Jupiter the gas giant whose immense gravitational field robbed the Red Planet of much of its potential material and mass as it formed.

Deep, deep below their crusts both planets were still liquid-hot. Water trapped beneath ground boiled up from the depths, evaporating into the atmosphere. Over time mighty oceans grew from the cooling rain that fell from the heavens onto the naked rocks; raging torrents that hammered over both naked, newly formed lands. But Earth was the one where mighty oceans grew, filling deep rocky basins with plentiful water. On Mars, broad shallow lakes formed. However, over the course of time, like life itself subjected to entropy, they faded away into the thin, cold atmosphere or sank below the surface of the land.

Earth with its large glistening oceans took on a blue tint, but Mars gradually turned into a dusty windy desert, its waters hidden deep beneath its ground. The Martian world turned rust-red, a cold reddish desert, bleak and hostile with an atmosphere that was predominately 95 percent carbon dioxide, 3 percent nitrogen, and 1.5 percent argon with minimal traces of oxygen and water.

Then a time of silence came... Evolution favoured the Earth and caused life to arise on the blue planet. The seas were filled with life in abundance. Over time this life overspilled and the land became the realm of roaming beasts rising up and dying out in waves of evolution and extinction events. Eventually Man came into being, sharing and striving to dominate the land of the wild beasts, complex organic life like neurotoxic snakes, vipers of countless kinds, crocodiles, tigers, lions, elephants, insects such as ants and bees and so forth. But as time elapsed Man's intelligence, his ability to communicate in the abstract and his grasping of technology allowed him to survive and weather such perils until Modern Man reached soaring heights. As evolution led life from the oceans to the land, technological scientific advancements led Mankind into outer space and eventually to Mars. In reaching the Red Planet they conquered it in all its fullness.

The terraforming process was a huge success. It entailed thickening the Martian atmosphere and allowing water to exist on the surface in liquid form. Greater sunlight absorption was the key. Heating the planet via orbital mirrors reduced the planet's albedo and in turn released carbon dioxide into the atmosphere creating a green-house effect. Over time, a human friendly atmosphere was produced. In addition, comets and asteroids were redirected so that they would crash into the planet's surface releasing their gases into the thin Martian atmosphere, generating huge amounts of heat. Another technique involved pumping out huge amounts of greenhouse gases, such as ammonia and methane. Over the course of time this helped thicken the Martian atmosphere.

The importation and introduction of algae was another integral part of the terraforming project. Algae broke down carbon dioxide which in turn produced oxygen. It helped lower Mars's albedo further by trapping more of the Sun's heat rather than reflecting it back into space. As the temperature and pressure on Mars increased it allowed all the frozen water to melt, forming lakes and rivers. Mars it turned out had vast amounts of water frozen as ice, both in its polar caps as well as underground, all the way down to the mid-latitudes.

The weather on Mars was bizarre to Earth eyes. Many of the early colonists saw tornadoes that were several miles high and hundreds of metres wide. This in turn created miniature lightning bolts as the dust and sand within become electrically charged. The early colonists also had to adjust to a much weaker gravitational field. As Mars's gravity is around 38% that of Earth it was hard to retain a human friendly atmosphere on the planet. The atmosphere was in danger of being lost to outer space. But this was overcome by keeping the temperature of the planet warm and by replenishing the atmosphere.

There was one thing however that terraforming could not rectify. The problem of cosmic radiation from outer space was a result of the lack of a magnetic field due to the slowing of the planet's iron centre, its magnetic core.

Billions of years ago, Mars was once a very different place. Like Earth, Mars had a planetary magnetic field generated by action in its core. But when that field disappeared, things changed drastically on the planet. This forced the colonists to live in large, shielded habitats, huts which protected them from the harmful radiation such as gamma rays and ultraviolent light. The indoor city centres on Mars had to be built from special alloys which repelled these highly energetic particles.

In order to maintain this human-friendly atmosphere via terraforming, a giant magnetic shield was launched into space to protect Mars from solar winds which would eat away at the atmosphere. The magnetic shield acted as a replacement for Mars's own lost magnetosphere. This giant magnetic shield eliminated much of the solar wind erosion that occurred in the planet's ionosphere and upper atmosphere.

It takes Mars 687 Earth days to orbit the Sun. As its orbital path is not in sync with Earth's it goes through a 26-month cycle of being closest and furthest from the blue planet. Thus, the distance between Mars and Earth is variable, due to their elliptical orbits around the Sun. At their closest points the distance between these two celestial spheres equates to 35 million miles. This is known as opposition. At their furthest points, the distance equates to 249 million miles. This change in distance meant spacecraft destined for Mars were sent out in a launch window every 26 months, when Mars was closest to Earth. A special trajectory called the Hohmann transfer orbit was used. This worked because of a fundamental law in orbital mechanics which states that if you can increase a spacecraft's energy at perihelion, you can increase the aphelion of its orbit, which is how far it gets from the Sun. Furthermore, it was necessary to arrive in position in Mars's orbit around the Sun at the precise time that Mars itself did and such an alignment occurs only once every two years.

The journey from Earth to Mars, when the two are at their closest points, initially took around nine months. However due to a huge breakthrough in technology, nuclear thermal propulsion meant that journey was reduced to around two months. Man no longer had to wait for the planets to align. Launch opportunities were there every year. Engineers no longer had to rely on swinging around planets to get gravity boosts to provide the extra power needed to send space probes deep into the solar system. Using a nuclear thermal rocket allowed faster transit time, reducing risk during space travel. This was a key component for human missions to Mars, as longer trips required more supplies and more robust systems.

In a nuclear thermal rocket engine, a fission reactor to generate extremely high temperatures, and a liquid propellant, in this case hydrogen, were used. The process boiled down to splitting uranium atoms inside a reactor core and pumping liquid hydrogen through the reactor where the resulting heat from the fission was used to convert the hydrogen into a gas which under pressure was ejected through a nozzle, creating the thrust needed to propel a spaceship. There were other benefits to this form of space travel too including increased science payload capacity and higher power for instrumentation and communication. And thus it was that Mankind's long anticipated colonisation of Mars became a golden reality... a new dawn.

Chapter 2 – The Arrival

Approximately forty minutes earlier they had been in orbit around the Red Planet. Then came the frightening journey down as they burnt their way through the thin Martian atmosphere. The descent vehicle shook violently. The ride was bumpy until they finally reached the ground and on touchdown the rocket thrusters ceased. There was no sound. The four brave men, all scientists, sat in awestruck silence, encased in bulky silver-coloured pressure suits. Another two men sat in the cockpit above... pilot and co-pilot: a total of six men. It was a historic moment. Man had landed on a mysterious new world... a red, lonely desert with high levels of iron. Wind eroded surface rocks and soil, and ancient volcanoes blew out the iron, spreading it all over the planet. When this occurred, the iron within the dust reacted with oxygen producing the red rust colour.

Commander Allan Johansen could hear nothing through the thick insulation of his pressure suit helmet except his own erratic breathing tinged with both excitement and fear. Then, as one, safety harnesses were unstrapped and he and his men rose slowly, if somewhat uneasily from their chairs. It was a dizzy moment... In the cramped compartment of the descent vehicle there was only one observation port. During their descent that single window had become a blazing furnace of Martian air. Allan looked out of the small spherical window and gazed at the lonely landscape that was Mars. A cold, hostile desert that stretched as far as the eye could see with wind-shaped dunes, rocks, and reddish sand. Above them, the sky was a pinkish red. Allan started to think about the images he had seen of Mars whilst on Earth, making comparisons... Mars was far more spectacular in the flesh, he thought, far more. His face moved with emotion. He shut his eyes for a brief moment and could feel the enveloping presence of the other world... Mars...

"Wow," gasped Viktor Bessonov into his helmet microphone, as he pressed behind gazing through the window. He was the youngest one there, a dreamer, a joker at times. He said, "We are here, finally..."

"Yes," replied Allan. "You do realise that we have made history. Our landing represents a new dawn for Mankind."

"Indeed," muttered Evangelos Alexopoulos, known for his altruism, as he too pressed behind looking out. "We are here on another world." Then, ever practical he added, "much to do."

Allan suddenly began to think hard about the mission ahead... the new world that awaited them. He had given up his life in a sense. He had left it all behind. His earthly existence was for now, no more. He pictured the Earth's oceans, its majestic blue skies, tall, elaborate buildings and the brightly lit cities, the mountains... the Himalayas which he had seen during his travels, the steaming jungles that thrived with life. He stood there deep in thought, his eyes fixed towards the desolate landscape that was Mars. He became aware of Markovic pressing behind also eager to view their new home through the small window. He edged aside as much as he could to allow his colleague his first view of Mars.

Despite their eagerness to get on with the next phase of their mission, the first member of the crew to leave the landing ship was the well-built construction robot. The metal vehicle rolled across the Martian sand on its six springy wheels and then halted abruptly. They all squeezed into the observation port to watch the square-sided machine, reassured by the sight of the bulky but vitally important tanks of liquefied air fixed to its top. From the truck's front, metal arms smoothly unfolded without a hitch, gleaming wickedly in the Martian light. The arms began to pull a heap of plastic rubbery-looking material from the machine's side. Next, the robot expertly spread the shiny heap of plastic out on the rusty red sand and gradually filled it with air from the big tanks. The heap grew and slowly took shape becoming a rigid hemispherical dome. This inflated dome would be their home, the first human habitation on Mars.

"That's it!" said Allan trying to control the excitement in his voice. "It's almost ready for us. We'll get more equipment soon via the automated, unmanned one-way landers from the spacecraft in orbit."

They all looked on watching with anticipation as the robot slowly continued to build their inflated dome... To the four scientists it was as if time had ceased. They could see the robot fixing the dome's rim firmly to the soil. It worked on and on as you would expect a robot to do, its sensors sampling the thin air outside. Next, it fitted a second heavy metal airlock into the dome's structure.

"I can't wait to actually step outside, move our feet on the Martian soil," said Evangelos starting to fidget, his eyes wide and alert.

"Soon enough," replied Allan sensing his colleague's impatience. "But we must follow the mission plan as instructed. Let's wait till the dome structure is completely finished and pressurized."

While the scientists watched the robot build their home, the pilot Hans, and co-pilot Michael, both astronauts, were busy in the cockpit. Hans, tired yet still focused, checked out all the lander's systems while he meticulously reported to the mission leader in the spacecraft orbiting overhead. The mission leader would then relay the information to the mission controllers back on planet Earth... So far all had gone to plan. That done, Hans started to reflect on their journey to the Red Planet. It had been one heck of a journey... During their nine-month flight from Earth their spacecraft had spun on a five-kilometre-long tether to simulate a feeling of weight. On board the spacecraft their artificial gravity began at a normal planet Earth one g and was then gradually reduced during the tiring months of their flight to the Martian value of approximately one-third g. Prolonged periods in zero gravity were a serious health hazard. It demineralised bones and dangerously weakened muscles.

He shook off his reverie and then said, "Michael, you know we're going to need a twenty-four-month calendar here?

"Huh?" grunted the co-pilot.

Hans adopted his best 'condescending lecturer' voice. It was a sort of game they played to pass the time, trying to outdo each other with facts and figures. "Mars revolves around the Sun at an average distance of 228 million km... Thus, it takes the Red Planet approximately 686.98 Earth solar days to complete one orbit around the Sun. The average length of a Mars sidereal day is 24 hours, 37 minutes, 22.663 seconds. Thus, we will need a twenty-four-month calendar here..."

"Yes Hans," sighed Michael and then brightened. "Hey, maybe that's a good business opportunity. We could be Mars' first calendarians. He turned to look at his friend, suddenly serious. "I guess this is where the mission truly begins... our objectives, adjust, explore and eventually terraform..."

"You having second thoughts bud?" said Hans jokingly.

"What? No! I wouldn't miss this."

Michael's eyes suddenly became distant and reflective... He said, "I remember a helicopter ride with my father when I was nine years old. It's one of those really vivid memories, you know? He worked in the oil industry as a geophysicist. The big chopper clattered and lurched in the gusty wind. I recall glancing out the window, the glaring sunlight blinding me. At the time it was as if I had experienced the ultimate adventure, the ultimate ride one could have. But look at me now, years on... I'm on Mars... and I have sealed my name in history." A huge grin lit up his face and Hans returned it in spades.

Time passed slowly for the impatient explorers... but eventually all six were cooped up together around the airlock, with their backpacks chafing, bundled uncomfortably inside their hard-shell silver-coloured suits. Occasionally Allan would look through the window to see if the dome structure was ready for them, filled with breathable air. There were only four, fold-down seats in the cramped compartment of the airlock level of the descent vehicle. The cockpit sat above meaning both the pilot and co-pilot had to stand.

"Boy I can't wait to get out. It's suffocating in here and there's hardly any space to move. It was bad enough reaching Mars. Nine months from Earth and now this..." said Evangelos impatiently.

"We'll be out of here shortly," muttered Commander Allan. "Most of the space in here has been consumed with housing equipment and supplies. It was designed for efficiency not comfort. But remember, if we needed to, we could live for days inside the descent vehicle."

"I know, but I really hope that won't be the case," replied Evangelos grumpily.

"At least we have all remained sane." added Markovic. "Space psychosis was a real worry. I was told that it was highly probable given the journey, the mission at hand and the shortage of sensory stimuli."

"Well, I guess those exercise machines on board the ship were partly responsible for keeping that in check," said Viktor grinning. He had made good use of them and would have flexed his muscles if there had been room.

Still they waited. The six men assisted one another, making final vital checks. All the connections to the suit batteries, air regenerator and heater had to be carefully inspected. They checked and rechecked making sure all was in place and as it should be. The backpacks were designed to connect automatically to ports in the pressure suits. The smallest misalignment could be fatal out on the surface of the Red Planet. It would be an agonizingly painful death... The atmosphere, around 95 percent carbon dioxide, 3 percent nitrogen, and 1.5 percent argon with minimal traces of oxygen and water was a lethal unbreathable combination for any unprotected human traversing Mars' landscape. Nothing could be overlooked. Eventually though, everything was in order, including their flexible gloves and heavy boots.

"Okay, it's time," said Allan excitedly as he looked through the window. "The dome is ready." His heart was pounding hard.

Markovic, Evangelos, Hans, Michael and Viktor gave a thumbs up. There was a moment of silence, as if each man was suddenly overwhelmed by the fact that they were each about to fulfil their long-awaited dream and not just their own. Mankind had dreamt about this very moment throughout the ages, and they were the ones about to step outside the descent vehicle and plant their booted feet on Mars, the first men in history to reach the mysterious Red Planet, a planet scarred by huge geological features, canyons, sandy orange-red rugged craters, volcanoes, and infinite dunes. Ancient eyes had studied this planet, gazing at it in the night sky from Earth, wondering about its mysteries as it wandered through the stars.

They all slid the transparent visors of their helmets down and locked them in place. Allan stood by the metal hatch. With a gloved hand he finger-activated the air pumps and the light on the airlock control panel turned from green to amber. The pumps began to work, labouring away. Air was sucked out of the compartment. Suddenly the labouring pumps stopped and the indicator light on the panel close to the metal hatch went to dark red.

"Let's do this," muttered Hans, his Germanic accent accentuated by suppressed excitement.

"I'm ready," said Michael as if summoning courage.

Allan focused hard. It was as if he had momentarily disconnected his conscious mind from its bodily functions and other visual distractions. He pulled the lever. The metal hatch opened slightly. He calmly pushed on it until it was completely open and the landscape of Mars was fully displayed. All six men took a gulp of their suit's cold air. Like alien invaders from another world, they were ready for the mission at hand. Indeed, the six men on Mars were in fact alien invaders from another world...

Allan started down the ladder one booted foot at a time. Next came Hans, followed by Evangelos, then Viktor, Markovic and lastly Michael. Soon, six pairs of booted feet were firmly planted on the ground. The wind of Mars plucked at them gently, as if to welcome them, the pale distant sun shining.

As a pilot, Hans' initial instinct was to inspect the Lander. It had certainly done its job, a piece of engineering brilliance. Its ceramic-coated alloy had absorbed the monstrous heat of their historical entry into the Martian atmosphere. The ceramic underside of the aeroshell was blackened and streaked from its incandescent flight through the upper atmosphere. Piloting the Mars descent vehicle down to the surface was quite an experience. Hans thought briefly about the return journey. The Lander would eventually be used as an ascent vehicle, blasting them back into orbit around the planet. *'It's going to be an interesting trip home,'* he thought. He knew exactly what to expect. For a brief moment, he pictured it in his mind; one after the other, the three ascent modules lifting from the surface of Mars on tongues of shimmering flame... rocket engines blowing miniature sandstorms across the arid dry landscape as they departed, leaving the lower half of each lander/ascent vehicle sitting empty on the red, dusty Martian ground. He pictured it all as if it had already happened, and then dismissed it. They were going to be busy. He looked up gazing into the Martian atmosphere. Eventually team two, the second lander, would make their way down in re-entry trajectory...

The other five men gazed around in awe looking toward the dead horizon, the magnificent landscape, the giant volcanoes thrusting their massive cones high into the thin cold atmosphere as they had for untold millennia... the ocean of water frozen beneath the ground waiting for a warmer time when it could release its vital moisture and renew the Martian world once more, the pink-orange sky, a planet where the seasons were twice as long as earth's and everyday was forty minutes longer. The human biorhythm would be altered for all time. Mars had an axial tilt and a rotation period similar to those of Earth. This meant Mars experienced seasons: spring, summer, autumn, winter much like Earth. A summer day on Mars could get up to 20 degrees Celsius and at night the temperature could drop to -73 degrees Celsius.

Allan's first instinct was to blink and rub his eyes. But his gloved hands bumped into the transparent visor of his helmet. He grinned ruefully and thought... *'It's as dead here as the moon. Still, life adapts, under certain conditions. Organism and environment change together.'* He gazed at the lifeless rocks ahead. If he were to bring one of the rocks into the dome for study purposes, suddenly thrusting it into an alien environment, an Earth mix of oxygen and nitrogen would kill any native organisms that may be inside it. If Martian rock was to be examined, it would have to be kept in the Martian environment. His mind drifted back to when he was a child, a young teen reading sci-fi and fantasy, watching all those science fiction movies about the green Martians that inhabited the Red Planet. He smirked. *'There are no such things as Martians,'* he thought, gently amused by his younger self... at least that's how it seemed. Ironically it was those very things, the sci-fi magazines, books, and the movies which had ultimately catapulted him into becoming a man of science, and now a pioneer, one of the first men to reach Mars.

Via his helmet earphones Viktor could just about hear the Italian team leader Bernardino Romano conversing with the expedition commander, American Albert Schwarz up in the orbiting spacecraft. Bernardino's voice was full of boiling excitement. All that hard work to get them there... Viktor's mind began to travel back to when he, along with the others, were shuttled to the assembly station riding in low orbit three-hundred kilometres above the surface of the blue green planet Earth. He recalled the beautiful images that he saw from that altitude... the planet curved huge and mesmerizingly beautiful, overwhelming all human senses. He recalled the broad expanses of blue, the majestic oceans of Earth decked with gleaming white clouds, a planet thriving with life, glowing majestically against the black emptiness of space. The assembly station itself had been a composite habitat. Viktor and all the other scientists had lived and worked there for over a month before they departed for Mars, getting to know one another; social adaptation and space conditioning. He was mesmerised by the two long narrow Mars spacecraft gleaming wickedly white in the fiery sunlight as they hung in the emptiness of space a few hundred meters from the dull brown bulbous assembly station... the support workers in their white space suits hovering, transferring supplies and equipment every day.

Allan smiled to himself as he caught sight of Viktor lost in his thoughts. He could not blame the man in all honesty. It was a moment each of them would treasure in their own way. He walked over to the now motionless robot construction vehicle with low gravity steps, his boots stamping on the Martian soil, each step of historic significance. The backpack regenerator replaced carbon dioxide with oxygen that was breathable. But the filters and mini fans inside the well-designed suit could not remove all of the odours that accumulated. The suit had acquired that faintly acrid odour of his own body now. Working on, he checked the TV camera. It was sitting up at the front of the construction vehicle. Sweating like a labourer inside his pressurised hard suit and not really noticing his low-gravity strength, Allan turned around and said into his helmet microphone to the five men who were now all focused on him, "Right, it's all set, the TV camera is ready. The world, planet Earth will soon be able to see us here on the Martian surface... so get ready. We will all have to give a brief speech."

The five men immediately reacted, pride etched into their eyes. Hans and Michael began brushing dust off their suits. Evangelos was a little nervous. Both Viktor and Markovic stood there practising what they were going to say, after all it was a historic moment.

Commander Allan looked towards his men checking they were ready and then, looking towards the camera meters away, addressed the people of Earth,

"Greetings from Mars. We are the first six men to set foot on the planet... the second lander will soon follow. We scientists, space pioneers if you will, wanted to explore the universe and conquer Mars and now we are here. Many were against the idea. Many of the politicians said that the billions invested in such a project should be spent on education, housing, and sea exploration. But against all odds we got the nod, and we are now here thanks to a small number of highly influential politicians that worked frantically to get as many as possible to help fund the Mars Project. Our arrival here will serve as a stimulus to develop new technology all funded by government. And just like Christopher Columbus who traversed the Atlantic and discovered the new world, we will be remembered as the great space pioneers of our age... the first men to set foot on another planet... Many of our doubters want to see quick and spectacular results, but it will take time for us to terraform Mars and colonise this cold desolate landscape..."

Hours later, when all the speeches had been made... Allan stood alone outside the dome in the bitter cold, gazing into the atmosphere. The sun was almost on the horizon. The sky to the east was already dark. The tiny pale sun touched the flat horizon. The pink sky deepened to red, then a uniform violet as the sun dipped out of sight. A single ghostly wisp of a glowing cloud hung above the horizon momentarily. Then the sun vanished and the cloud dissipated into the all-encompassing darkness. The sky was shimmering, glowing faintly with flickering colours... an Aurora. The lights pulsed and billowed across the Martian sky... tantalizing pastels of pink, blue, green, and white... particles from the solar wind hitting the upper atmosphere, the gases up there glowing as particles excited them. Eventually the colours faded leaving the sky still and dark.

Through the tinted visor of his helmet, he saw the eternal stars, majestically bright and energetic, looking down at him. Even on an alien planet those familiar stars, the guardians of universal order were watching over him. It gave him a sense of hope, comfort, and belief that all would go to plan. Then, he noticed something moving across the sky. He wondered whether it was the ships in orbit but as he watched he realized it was the moon Phobos, so close, going from west to east. Deimos was too faint to see unless one knew exactly where to look for it. There was no discernible moonlight on Mars, its two satellites were too tiny to shed much light on the planet's surface. He then recognized Orion and Taurus, with the cluster of the Pleiades in the bull's neck. An amazingly glorious bright blue dot shimmering low on the horizon suddenly caught his eye.

"That's got to be Earth," he muttered to himself in reverence...

He stood there for a time absorbing the sight, an almost spiritual experience he had not expected. The blue sphere was far luckier than its red neighbour. It was closer to the Sun, that giant, life-giving nuclear reactor. Planet Earth thrived with life, from its oceans where great creatures took command of the sea, to the land where men dominated. On planet Earth the atmosphere absorbed any particles that powered through the magnetic field, so that even the most energetic solar flare would not endanger life on the surface. And in low Earth orbit astronauts were protected from solar flare particles by Earth's magnetic field which deflected the energetic protons and electrons and eventually pumped them down into the atmosphere at the north and south magnetic poles. Sadly, Mars lacked a magnetosphere due to the slowing of its magnetic core, which meant that the planet was subject to enormous amounts of lethal cosmic radiation. The Red Planet was poisonous, desolate... Enormous volcanoes reared their mighty peaks toward the flickering cold stars and spread hot lava and steaming gases over the face of the land. And there was still energy deep beneath the Red Planet's crust... molten energy to build the tallest mountains ever. How the two celestial spheres differed in terms of beauty. Earth was home to man... Mars was a dead, alien hostile world...

Allan turned on his helmet lamp, instantly destroying his night-adapted vision to make sure it was in working order. He then turned it off and gazed back into the night Martian sky and said to himself, "One day this will be home to Man as well, fully terraformed, with all its secrets exposed." With that, he turned and made his way back into the dome...

Chapter 3 – Terraformed Mars

Four hundred years after the first pioneers had stepped foot on Mars, Ivan Dobrovolski stood by the window inside his radiation protected hut, deep in thought. Early morning Martian sunlight streamed in through the spherical window. He was experiencing a mix of emotions, primarily excitement tinged with a little apprehension, as tomorrow was the day he had an appointment booked with the Philosophical Society. The irony was it was run by a team of robots. It had been a sudden decision following a live broadcast where he had seen one of the head robots dialoguing with another of its own kind. It said, "Consciousness is an interesting phenomenon. It lies partly in the psychological realm." Ivan grinned now, as he had during the live broadcast. What could a robot truly understand about the nature of consciousness? But this was the main reason why he made the appointment... curiosity the chief culprit.

Ivan pulled away from the window, walked over to his multi-coloured sofa, and sat, running a hand through his thick brown hair. Across the wall the vision set sprang into life, triggered by his faint motion. Reaching over to the sitting-room table, he picked up his glass of Martian tonic. It was a potent blend of liquids and finely ground special herbs. He raised the transparent glass and drank it down greedily. That same tantalizing buzz swept through him as it always did as the potent mixture mildly burnt his throat and stung his eyes. It allowed him to condense his dreams and scattered thoughts into a semblance of rationality.

He placed the empty glass on the table and grabbing at the glittering silver remote began to search the channels. A news bulletin caught his attention. He raised the volume until it was clearly audible... A well- dressed newswoman, clad in the uniform of her profession, tailored suit, well-coiffed hair, full lips sealed with vivid lipstick, was making a statement. Her serene and calming voice gave a lie to the alarming content of that statement. Being a journalist in his own right Ivan was well aware that this news channel was merely an arm of the government propaganda machine, but he listened anyway.

"All citizens should note that the Governing Leaders of Mars have brought in a new law which comes into immediate effect. All citizens of Mars are now required to have the encephalic nano-chip implant. It is a quick painless procedure where the chip, which will reduce and prevent crime and ultimately protect society, will be inserted into the brain. The final decision was taken yesterday by Supreme Leader, Roger J. Locke."

Roger J. Locke's wise and benevolent face now filled the screen. He said... "All the citizens of Mars now have a bright future, a new beginning, a new dawn. This nano-chip is divine in nature and will be used to protect all civilians on Mars."

The well-dressed newswoman returned to the screen: "As of now, no one may leave the planet until all civilian citizens of Mars have had the implant. Once the programme is completed, travel will resume as normal. Implantation centres are open in all areas and will provide this service on a walk-in basis so there is no need to book an appointment. Each citizen will be informed when it is their turn to come forward. The whole procedure will take only five minutes and has been extensively tested on the prison population with no adverse effects reported. Once travel from the planet resumes, every Mars citizen can be proud that we are leading the way and will be the most respected of visitors as our individual minds will still be monitored regardless of where we may be. The people of Mars will be revered throughout the solar system."

Ivan hit the mute button in shock. He had heard rumours about this before and it concerned him greatly. This was mind control. This had nothing to do with reducing crime and protecting the Martian citizens. This was a clever strategic move from the

Governing Leaders to convince the masses that it was for their good. He could not quite believe what he was hearing. He started to reach for his Martian tonic, needing something to slow his jumbled thoughts but stopped when he caught sight of his anguished face in the glass tabletop. He needed to think and feel everything as it came right now. Even self-induced chemical mind control seemed inadvisable at this point. The Governing Leaders of Mars who promoted themselves as an elite group of brilliant minds controlled the Martian system and now, they were bringing in a law that would essentially steal the souls of the Martian inhabitants. He looked back at the vid screen and turned the sound back up. The news anchor had been replaced by the young enthusiastic technology reporter, Steve Knight.

"These special nano-chips will be used to monitor the minds of all the citizens of Mars. Now for those of you with a technical bent this next bit is really interesting. Hacking into the brain requires decoding the logic of neurons. In the same way the human genome was decoded by scientists back on earth centuries ago. Mars' greatest minds have been working on this for many years and now we can all benefit from the fruits of their labour. As a result of this tiny chip," a picture of a small silicone square replaced his smiling face on the screen, "crime will decrease and can even be prevented. Don't worry though, this image you're seeing on your screen now was captured by the most powerful electron microscope on Mars. Millions of these will fit on a single typed full stop on a page. You'll never know it's there." His grinning face returned to the screen as he continued, "Once the nano-chip has been carefully implanted into the brain it has the capacity to store all encephalic data, all thoughts, feelings, and emotions. Signals which are sent out from a satellite in space will collect all the registered information on the nano-chip, all brainwave activity. It will be then registered on a giant supercomputer. Again, don't worry, this information can only be accessed by personnel authorised by the government. It will not be for public consumption. Everything will be monitored. Now back to the science."

Ivan had in the past found this young-looking fair-haired reporter's style rather entertaining, but now the over-enthusiastic explanations and reassurances sent chills down his spine. This was science, yes, but it was heavily slanted by propaganda. He liked his science pure and factual so he could assess the information and draw his own conclusions.

"...Thoughts are energy signals. The energy transmitting a thought therefore has mass. The ions and molecules encoding the energetic signal have mass too. Since thoughts are physical and have spatial dimension, it is now possible to 'lock-in' and read a person's thoughts via brain wave patterns – neuronal activity. Some thoughts are consolidated as memories. Memory too is a physical process, encoded by structural molecular changes in neuronal connections..."

Ivan switched the channel. He'd had enough. He knew what the implications were: the future here on Mars would be a planet of mind-controlled cattle. He shook his head as if trying to clear away the horrid subject within. He lay back on the sofa and for a few minutes tried to meditate, eyes closed. After all there was nothing he could do to change things. Minutes later, unable to relax, he reopened his eyes and flicked through the channels once again. This time something else caught his attention. It was a documentary about the terraformation and colonisation of Mars. This was soothing to him. He loved history and science. Ivan focused on the screen trying to forget about the implications of the nano-chip which sadly continued to roam in the depths of his mind. He had always been fascinated with the subject of terraforming and the historic men that were responsible for colonising the planet. The narrator spoke passionately, smoothly, elegantly, with a tinge of awe:

"These were the first six brave men to set foot on the surface Mars: Scientists Allan Johansen, Hans Ziegler, Evangelos Alexopoulos, Viktor Bessonov, Markovic Majewski and Michael Archer. Everything about the Mars expedition was done in pairs and these great men specialised in robotics, engineering, biology, astrophysics, geology, architecture, physics, mathematics, geophysics, meteorology, geochemistry, and so forth. Now at that time, the two Mars craft had to be launched out of Earth orbit through a window at a certain time and in a precise direction with exactly the proper velocity. Once they were on their way, destination Mars, tiny cold-gas thrusters would spurt in a precisely programmed order and the spacecraft would begin to spin in an impressive, elegant rotation. The tethers would stretch to their full five-kilometre length. Inside the connected Mars spacecraft, a feeling of normal gravity would return. Astronomical telescopes and high-energy radiation sensors were carefully placed at the midpoint of the long tethers, where they would be effectively weightless and could maintain precise pointing accuracy for the brilliant astronomers who would expertly operate them remotely from the blue planet, Earth. Now remember, the journey to Mars back then had been a nine-month journey in interplanetary space, but due to nuclear thermal propulsion this journey from Earth to Mars only took around two months, as such journeys do to this very day..."

Ivan listened in fascination. The historical words of Allan Johansen followed in archaic fashion in ripples of visual static:

"The conquest of Mars has been the greatest achievement in human history thus far. Mars is the symbol of Man's burning desire to expand and explore this mysterious universe of ours. How can I describe this desolate planet to the people of Earth? Well, picture the Sahara Desert which is in the continent of Africa. Now remove every trace of life... Remove the lizards, chameleons, skinks and cobras that are found among the rocks and dunes. Now freeze-dry the entire landscape and plunge it down to a temperature of around a hundred below zero sucking away the air. Well, that is what Mars is like, the fourth planet out from the sun. However, this Red Planet, a desolate dry desert of sandy iron oxides, rusty iron dust, will via terraforming eventually become home to Mankind. There is water here. Mars has polar caps composed partially of frozen water, covered over most of the year by frozen carbon dioxide. In summary, Mars is a dead world, the complete opposite to Earth where life has crawled into every crevice and corner it can find. Even in the dry Antarctic deserts there is life hidden, concealed inside the rocks. But we are here to change that and when we succeed a new chapter will open for Mankind!"

Next the voice of the narrator returned against a backdrop of still pictures showing the men at work:

"One of the first things these brave pioneers, these scientists did was to collect contingency samples of the Martian rocks, soil, and of course atmosphere. As for the meticulously built construction robot... it moved across the Martian sands and rocks out to the three unmanned cargo carriers, scattered over a three-kilometre-wide radius from their nominal landing site. This fabulously constructed robot expertly hauled their cargos back to the inflated dome. This dome was now home for these six brave space pioneers and the electric power that heated the dome came from the compact nuclear generator inside one of the cargo vehicles... The dome's strong, plastic skin was double walled - well insulated to keep out the biting cold. Of course, it was filled with breathable air at normal Earth pressure and temperature making it viable for the six pioneers. A polarizing electric current which darkened the dome's skin kept heat inside. During Martian daylight, the inflated dome's lower section could be made transparent... the reason for this... to take advantage of solar gain. To combat the deadly radiation, the highly energetic particles, gamma rays and UV light, the topmost section of the dome was opaque. It was filled in with special dense plastic that would absorb damaging radiation. It even stopped small meteorites from puncturing through."

'Those early days!' thought Ivan smiling with pride. He was a proud Martian citizen, born and bred. The narrator's voice faded to silence, but the images continued to roll. Across the tele-set Ivan could see images of the historic dome. It was expertly laid out with two airlocks on opposite sides of its circular perimeter. All the life-support equipment was in the centre. He could see some tables of light-weight plastic. He could also see a communications centre. A longish white table set against one partition held analysis equipment and computer modules. Display screens flickered orange and blue, showing curves and graphs of data from the global network of sensors that changed every few seconds. He could also see the geology lab, an area partitioned off from the rest of the dome. A thin bearded geologist sat in a reclining chair in front of a computer display screen sipping tea from a delicate porcelain cup waiting for it to work its calming magic. Shelves were stacked with bare rocks and transparent plastic cases that held core samples and stoppered bottles filled with red Martian soil. He could see the men unloading the supplies from the lander – a magnificent vehicle. The men were carrying them from the airlock to their proper storage places inside the inflated air-filled dome. The air inside was an Earth-normal mix of oxygen and nitrogen, pumped up to normal terrestrial pressure and heated to a comfortable temperature. As for the

hard suits... they operated at almost normal terrestrial atmospheric pressure.

Next, across the tele-set screen he could see a dot, a formless dark blur in the Martian sky hurtling towards the surface. It was the second historic lander making its way down. It fell across the pink sky like a stone, dragging a bright flaming contrail behind it. Then a streak of colour majestically streamed from the top of the speck and billowed into a trio of white parachutes. The descent vehicle slowed, but it was still falling fast, swaying a little, gliding toward the surface of Mars with the three huge parachutes spread above it. Suddenly the parachutes separated from the descent vehicle, the lander. The chutes flapped away aimlessly with forgotten importance, drifting across the cold Martian world. Ivan looked on totally engrossed... the descent vehicle appeared to stagger in mid-air, puffs of greyish-white steam spurting from its control jets. The retrorockets accurately fired fitful short bursts, blasting grit and swirling dust. Finally, it landed, all intact...

Next the programme showed old footage of some of the scientists making their way into the dome, suits and equipment smudged with red dust. Mission protocol dictated that they should always carefully clean their suits and all their gear before stepping into the main section of the inflated dome. And that they did religiously. The area just inside the airlock, where the outside equipment and hard suits were stored, served as the clean-up and maintenance section. Ivan watched one of the scientists vacuuming the Martian dust from his boots with a little hand-held machine. One of the men, finally free of his hard suit, was sitting on a bench, hands on knees, silent, deep in thought. Another was preparing for an interview, sitting on a plastic chair in front of the main communications screen. Each of the explorers, these space pioneers, was expected to respond to the news media's demands for interviews... live, from Mars. Mission control would set it up. At this point in the mission, with the distance from Earth growing greater every hour, due to both planet's elliptical orbits around the sun, it took nearly ten minutes for a radio or TV transmission to travel from one celestial body to the other, thus live interviews were not possible. The producers and the world's audiences were accustomed to this fact, after all these brave men were on another planet.

The narrator's voice returned. "Early missions to Mars were timed for a period of low solar activity. However, there was only the slimmest of chances that a spacecraft could carry their human crews through nine months in space without running into a magnetic storm spawned by a solar flare. At the underground base on the airless moon, Luna,

Earth's natural satellite, with its minuscule magnetic field, solar forecasters would expertly watch the giant nuclear reactor that is the Sun, in cramped narrow workrooms... humming computers and video monitors everywhere. On planet Earth too, teams of forecasters would skilfully monitor the Sun. Their instruments could detect weak radio emissions and bursts of soft X rays from the sunspot group. But when a flare erupted all hell would break loose. To the eye it was nothing spectacular, just a brief flash of light. X ray and Ultraviolet sensors aboard monitoring satellites would go into overload. You see, a solar flare, a cloud of subatomic particles blown into space could kill unprotected humans within a matter of seconds. These highly energetic particles, a vast expanding cloud of energetic protons and electrons can literally slice through the shell of the ship and consume human flesh almost instantly. Solar forecasters' instruments automatically radioed a warning to the Mars spacecraft as it journeyed through interplanetary space, millions and millions of kilometres away from Earth. The electromagnetic radiation from the solar flare which travels at the speed of light just as the astronomers' radio signals did, hit the spacecraft at the same instant that the warnings arrived."

'Fascinating,' thought Ivan rubbing his jaw. He switched off the tele-set and dropped the remote

beside him. It had been a rewarding watch. Most of the Martian public were not too interested in these matters from the distant past, no matter how relevant they seemed, but for him it was a great education to understand how Mars became Mars, his home, his world. Ivan had not had a great education, most of what he knew was down to his own research, and he had done much. As a working journalist research was not alien to him. Although born on the Martian world, he felt as human as any Earthling... He had never lost that sense of humanity despite that fact he was born on the planet and had never gone to Earth to visit the home of his ancestors.

His mind now returned to the alarming fact that the citizens of Mars would now have to have a nano-chip implanted in their brains. What would those six pioneers think of that? He wondered when it would be his turn. He rubbed his jaw in thoughtful concern then dismissed the matter... at least for now. Tomorrow morning at 10:30 am he had his appointment with the Mars Philosophical Society. Many Martian citizens would meet with these robots... AI... and spend vast amounts of time engaging in deep conversation. In terms of communication, the robots were more human than human but their cold metallic structures were a constant reminder to all that they were nothing but well programmed machines.

There was a double knock at the front door. For some reason all his visitors tended to ignore the small bright door-buzzer, preferring instead the old-fashioned way. *'There might be an article in that,'* he thought idly as he made his way to the cream-coloured door. A well-dressed man stood there, short blond hair and dark eyes the colour of coal. Behind, parked on the dusty road was a black well-polished surface vehicle.

"Orson, it's been a while my friend, come in..." greeted Ivan, a little concerned by the serious look on his friend's face.

Orson stepped in and replied, "I was passing this way so thought I would come and see you. I can literally only stay a few minutes though."

They made their way through the small vanilla scented, yellow-coloured corridor, to the sitting room area and sat, Martian sunlight filtering into the cosy room that was peppered with paintings fixed to the wall, paintings by famous artists done the Martian way.

"So, Orson, how are you doing...? I've not seen you in around two months?"

"Yes, it's been that long." He scratched his forehead and then the tip of his pointed nose, a sign he was upset about something. "In terms of how I'm doing, well let's say I'm concerned, very concerned about our government and the way things are evolving politically. I thought Earth had its political problems and warped government officials but things here are getting really bad!"

Suddenly it clicked! Ivan knew why his friend had suddenly and unexpectedly turned up at his door.

"The chip... the new law... right?"

They looked at each other, eyes wide and open.

"Yes Ivan... The Governing Leaders... that so-called elite group of brilliant minds!"

"To be honest Orson," sighed Ivan, "I'm deeply concerned myself. I just saw the announcement this morning on the news."

"Me too, on my vid-screen in my surface-vehicle whilst driving... If I hadn't had it on autopilot, I'd have crashed it. The news cut through me like a knife. I can't believe it."

"Well let's be honest, they have been speaking about this chip for some time now with a great deal of enthusiasm, but I never thought that they would make it absolute law... I mean they're proposing that these brain implants are forced into the brains of all the citizens of Mars. When I first heard about it, I imagined that they would slowly make it available to the public and that the citizens of Mars could freely choose whether they wanted it or not with no obligation. But now the government, the iron hand, will force everyone to have it regardless."

"Yuk," blasted Orson. "The mere thought of having a chip working away inside me like some evil alien is quite frankly sickening. These damn nano-chips can monitor our brains, our minds, as if it were an entity of its own with powers beyond."

"Hacking into the brain requires decoding the logic of neurons Orson, and these damn scientists have done a bloody good job, sadly for us. Once the nano-chip has been implanted it has the capacity to store all encephalic data. Terrifying thought that."

"Indeed... and what really bugs me is how they are selling it to the masses, as if it will benefit the citizens of Mars, and society as a whole and the future of the Martian world. Their main punch line is... 'Crime will decrease and can even be prevented'. "

"I know Orson... clever mind mechanics involved here, but I'm sure there are many out there that won't buy into this nonsense. Don't get me wrong it could be that through the nano-chip crime will decrease and maybe even prevented in some cases... but in exchange for what? Ours souls... We will have to give up our souls for the cause, lose our identity, and become prisoners within. To hell with that...!"

"Absolutely Ivan," agreed Orson vehemently... Essentially speaking, we will become organic robots, mind-controlled... The future of Mars and its citizens is in serious jeopardy my friend. I dread the day when I'll be called in. I don't know what we are going to do. There seems to be no escape. The Martian government is nothing other than an all-powerful, malevolent force..."

"I agree... but we are not the only planet with that problem. Take Earth, their government toys with the minds of its inhabitants in many different ways. And they too have the nano-chip, but it isn't forced on the public like it will be here. The citizens of Earth have a choice, at least for now. We don't."

Ivan paused. There was a tense silence. Across his face dim sunlight shone. Orson too was lost in his own thoughts.

At last Ivan broke the silence and letting the words roll from his mouth, his eyes distant and reflective, he said, "When I'm called up for the implant it will be essentially like walking into a death chamber... walking out like the living dead. I don't know if there is an escape angle Orson, but if there is one, I will find it..."

Orson did not reply but looked him straight in the eye as if searching for something. Then he nodded, rose from the sofa and smiled ruefully.

"I've got to head off now. But let's keep in touch. I will see myself out."

They shook hands, a firm shake, and Orson made his way for the door...

Darkness had descended over the face of the Red Planet. It was night. Ivan sat alone in the amber gloom of a bar, the overhead light emitting a variation of colours that shone across his face in a quasi-orderly pattern. Jazz music played in the background. He found his mind flowing with the thread of the melody. He raised his dazzling glass of whiskey and Martian fruit juice and drank. He then placed it back on the table, idly stirring it with the plastic straw, watching the cubes of ice move clumsily about. Two things were uppermost in his mind, competing for his attention. Firstly, his discussion with Orson and the menacing chip, second, tomorrow's wonderful encounter with the robots of the Philosophical Society. But the weight and tormenting worry that came with the fact that all the citizens of Mars were now going to become nothing but organic robots, was taking its toll. One by one each Martian citizen would have their brains invaded with this nano-chip that worked away like a living entity, absorbing one's soul, extracting all encephalic data, thoughts, feelings, and emotions. It was essentially a form of digital possession. As far as he was concerned this was the end for Mars. The implications were vast and devastating. *'Something needs to be done to stop this,'* he thought bitterly but he found no answers in the whiskey glass.

Around him couples and groups ate and drank merrily, some nodding their heads to the music, murmuring away casually. Ivan absorbed bits of it here and there, still toying with the straw. *'Everyone seems happy enough,'* he thought and that worried him. This was a tiny indication that the Martian citizens were not troubled by the news. *'Perhaps I'm looking too deeply into this,'* he suddenly thought as he gazed around. Then he heard a suavely dressed young man speaking to his girlfriend, holding her hand as she sipped away at her drink.

"The Martian government knows best Sarah. Besides it will decrease crime, maybe even prevent it. I think it's rather exciting, this whole philosophy behind transhumanism embodied by a tiny nano-chip."

'Blast, I knew it,' Ivan thought, his face suffused with reddish anger. "It seems the government has already brainwashed the masses, either that or everyone is stupid," he muttered to himself bitterly. He stopped his introspection and stood in the amber gloom. Rapidly he made his way over to one corner. He halted beside the tele-set-screen. Across the wall was a glass-framed collection of worms... life forms from Earth which had been collected and taken to Mars as intriguing decor. They were all dead of course, unable to survive the journey. His eyes grew tired, his mind wandering as he looked apathetically at the collection. He took out his dial-card and inserted it into the slot and dialled. The line buzzed as the circuit was established. Orson's face appeared across the screen, bright and clear.

"How's it going?" said Orson as he looked at Ivan across his home tele-set- screen.

"I'm in the Olympus bar... needed to step out for a bit. I'll be heading back shortly. Tomorrow, I have an appointment with the Philosophical Society, 10:30 am."

"I didn't know you were going there. You never mentioned it to me this morning when I came by."

"Well, I am. Got curious so I thought I'd give it a go. Anyway, I wanted to speak to you Orson." He looked over his shoulder, then back to the screen. "It seems to me from what I've overheard in the bar that the masses are not too troubled by the new law, the chip, etc..."

"Yes, I know," Orson muttered, his voice tense. "After I saw you today, I went to see some relatives of mine. I spoke to them about what's happening. They were very defensive arguing that this is the best way forward for the citizens of Mars. I couldn't get a word in. I even bumped into a few friends, and they are all for it too. I don't get it. How can they all be so blind?"

Ivan looked over his shoulder, his forehead slightly sweaty and saw a lady walking over toward him, probably wanting to use the tele-set-screen.

"Look Orson it is best we cut here. I will contact you tomorrow after my meeting with the robots."

"Okay..."

The call cut sharply. Regaining his composure, he made his way back over to his table and sat... the bar and the gaudy opaque shapes of people fading before him into a meaningless blur. He finished his drink with a gulp, and waved over to the pretty brunette mutant waitress who had an extra thumb on her right hand. He paid leaving a handsome tip and left. All the bars and restaurants on Mars expected abnormally huge tips from all citizens especially tourists, a necessary lubricant in order to get first class service.

As he made his way over to his surface vehicle, hover-cars flashed across the night sky above him, humming softly. Neon lights flashed, flickered and pulsed. On the dusty street Martian citizens moved around in a circuitry of motion, some of them mutants. Many of the colonists had suffered the consequences of exposure to cosmic radiation. Sadly, many of the mutants were victims of prejudice. *'These crowds will all soon become mind-controlled zombies, the living dead,'* he thought.

It did not take long for him to reach his grey surface vehicle, the cold Martian wind circling about him. He pulled out the activator and with the press of a button the door flipped open, and Ivan clambered inside, latching the safety belt on... He consulted the chronometer that was fixed to the dashboard: It read 23:00. It was getting very late. Then he picked up the small can of weak beer that lay on the front seat next to him. He gulped it down quickly, wiped his mouth, catching his breath. Opening the window, he casually tossed it into the nearby bin, along with the day's anxieties. With a sharp command the surface vehicle hummed into life, and he drove smoothly away, heading for home...

It was the morning of a new day, the burning orb of the sun beaming down across the landscape of Mars. Ivan sat in a cab on his way to the Philosophical Society. He couldn't be bothered to drive himself. For a brief moment he gazed into the terraformed Martian sky. It was blue, similar to Earth's... As light passed through the air, its molecules scattered the blue light. *'How the great, great grandchildren of the first colonists got to enjoy the blue skies of a terraformed Mars,'* he thought merrily. Ivan had spent the journey so far reading a science-history book, titled... The Early Days on Mars... One scientist, Ben R. Bradbury recorded an incident when his dome was punctured.

'As I slowly walked back to my dome the ground around me suddenly erupted into puffs of dust. I was completely taken aback, startled. Then something banged on my helmet, a light tap but it concerned me. Then I noticed that the dome ahead was dimpling here and there as meteoroids struck. A burning intense fear of one of them breaking through threatened to overwhelm me, and sadly, one did, and it was the first time. As I rushed over a little geyser of spray erupted into the dry thin Martian atmosphere. The hole spread into a horrible growing rip as moisture-laden air geysered out into the thin, poisonous, toxic atmosphere of Mars, and the plastic fabric of the dome began to sag. The meteoroid that powered through both layers of the plastic must have been no bigger than a microscopic grain of dust. As I quickly entered the damaged dome everyone was rushing frantically for their suits. I could feel the breeze as the dome's air rushed toward the now gaping puncture. The terrifying hissing noise grew louder by the second, a rushing torrent of precious air. I attempted to repair the widening hole with repair patches, but they would not stay. The dome's air roared as it rushed into the near-vacuum outside. Soon it will be all gone, I thought desperately. The sheer force of the escaping wind tugged at me and the others trying to suck us through the wall and out into the arid open. I struggled hard against it, as did they. It was utter chaos...hellish! Chairs were scattered across the floor, a blizzard of loose papers flying, swirling through the dome. As for the life-support equipment... Boy this was absolutely vital. Pumps that gleefully sucked in the dry cold air of the Martian world... Separators that culled the minimal nitrogen and even scantier oxygen out of the native cold Martian atmosphere... More pumps to make the wonderful nitrogen/oxygen mix thick enough for human beings to breathe. I had to reach the oxygen, the oxygen tanks, stored there in case of emergency. And this I did, twisting their valves frantically until fully open, over-pressurising the dome as promptly as I could with pure oxygen. We eventually won the battle. We managed to repair the area of the dome where the meteoroid had broken through with repair patches and a special spray.'

"What are you reading there, buddy?" asked the cabdriver, as he battled with pockets of traffic, the speeding surface-vehicles, elaborate and slick.

Ivan closed the book and placed it on the seat. "It's a science-history book... The Early Days on Mars..."

"Not many Martian citizens' today are bothered with all that. Not to mention that books are scarce these days."

"Well, I've always been fascinated with Mars, our planet, the science and early history, and how it ultimately became what it is today. Plus, you can't beat a good hard book."

Ivan cut off and now looked out of the window watching the large elaborate indoor city domes, and spectacular triangular buildings shimmering in the Martian light. He was looking forward to his discussion with one of the robots. He was curious... very curious. The cab was entering the main city centre, Nova Colorado, reducing velocity. It was named after the American state Colorado, the home state of Allan Johansen, the commander of the original terraforming mission. Many of the cities on Mars were named after states and cities down on Earth.

The streets were busy with sound and activity despite the fact that Martian citizens tended to avoid going out and being exposed to cosmic radiation, preferring instead to stay inside the large indoor city domes built from special alloys. These special alloys repelled the dangerous radiation. The lack of a magnetosphere was the problem, no protection against cosmic radiation. The slowing of Mars' iron magnetic core was responsible.

Mars had been a puritanical culture in years past, but much had changed. Sex bars, as they were known, were many. Martian citizens casually roamed around dressed in their well-designed multicoloured clothes, some still struggling to take in the thin weak air of the colonised world. But the days of carrying one's portable oxygen were long gone, over for centuries. Mars was alive, Martian insects crawling and buzzing. A holographic advertisement flashed into life. Brilliant images of Earth appeared an augmented reality. It was a holiday advertisement: 'CHEAP FLIGHTS TO EARTH.' Many would rush to the blue planet. Two of its main attractions were the Amazon Jungle famed for its incredible wildlife, and Mount Kilimanjaro located in Tanzania in the continent of Africa. But it wasn't easy for the citizens of Mars to adjust to Earth's strong gravity. Conversely, many of the Earthlings that visited Mars would want to see Olympus Mons, the enormous shield volcano, over 72,000 ft high, which was located in Mars' western hemisphere.

"Okay, we are here," said the cabdriver breaking through his reverie. The cab dropped speed with a sudden jolt, then it halted. It was parked a few meters away from the dome.

Ivan checked his watch. It read 10:28 am. *'Perfect,'* he thought. He looked up and saw the beautiful dome, the one he had seen countless times before but never really took much interest in, until recently when he had suddenly decided to go and meet with the robots for the small sum of 300 Martian credits. It had all been prepaid days before. He was ready...

Ivan inspected the small screen which lay above the credit register of the cab. It was neatly positioned, fixed to the inner structure of the surface vehicle at the back. The sum owing was displayed across the screen in green digits: 3o Martian credits. Ivan pulled out his silver-metallic card from his jacket and fed it into the credit register. Within a matter of seconds, the register buzzed signalling credit taken.

"That's it, thank you buddy," said the driver. "Have a good day."

The back door slid open smoothly. Ivan grabbed his book and stepped out. In front of the dome, a Mars-Earth Distance Indicator flashed and a softly spoken female voice spoke, 'Current distance between Mars and Earth: 35 million miles - 56 million km. From the information given Ivan knew that Mars and Earth were at their closest points. Most Martian citizens loved to be informed of such information, after all sister Earth was the planet from where all life had originally sprung into being.

Ivan stood awkwardly inside the dome holding his book. Strangely no one was to be seen. His eye was drawn to the middle of the great hall, which was graced by a large, elegant, triple bowl fountain. It looked like something that belonged on Earth. The sound of discharging, running water had a calming effect. It was rather pleasing to the eye he decided. The great hall was filled with statues and sculptures. Everything seemed to ooze class and elegance. It was as if he had been teleported to another world. Even the air inside seemed to have its own mysterious scent. Then he noticed the words which were etched into one of the walls in gold: '**Objective reality is built upon the foundation of a multitude of subjective realities which in turn form a universal concept.**'

Suddenly across the Great Hall a team of robots emerged from a large pale blue door, walking toward the fountain, fine, slender and metallic. Ivan found it a little odd. No one had greeted him, and it seemed he was being ignored. The robots sat around the fountain just like the ancient Greek philosophers of old would have down on Earth, conversing, their undulating arms weaving inquiringly as they communicated with one another. Then one of them broke free from the team and slowly, elegantly walked over towards Ivan. Ivan studied its motion carefully. He was well informed in robotics, and the mechanics that went into building such machines. 'When this robot walks, it uses infrared and ultrasonic sensors to gauge distances from floors, walls and moving objects. It constantly adjusts its balance and motion with 34 high – precision servo motors. It is equipped with an internal gyroscope and speed sensor that helps it achieve balance. Special sensors regulate the amount of force that it applies depending on the task at hand. This robot is truly one of the greatest examples of what science has achieved. It represents engineering, physics and mathematics all rolled into one. And robots don't have millions of years of evolution and social cognition like humans, and yet in some ways they exceed us. In narrow categories, machines exceed human brilliance by a distance, and that's why I'm here,' he concluded.

Reaching Ivan it said, "Greetings, Sir. You must be Ivan Dobrovolski."

"I am indeed."

The robot's voice was soft and refined, more human than human.

"I'm Alexis. Please follow me Sir..."

He was led to a magnificent, brightly lit room on ground level. There was a large white table there. In the centre of this table was a grey bowl containing various fruits. Next to it was a large brown jug filled with red wine and a tall empty glass. Ivan found this rather amusing but very impressive. It was a casual setting. He had not expected this. He was taken aback. The room itself looked like the inside of a mini Greek temple. Printed across the chalk white wall in black were the words: **Existence is mass energy and motion in space time. To be is to resonate.** He knew that he was certainly in the right place.

Classical music played in the background, Mozart. The Martian citizens loved music, especially classical and the great composers from Earth. Ivan focused once again on the machine. From an aesthetic point of view, it was just a bundle of well-organised metal and plastic, with a nonhuman nervous system, but it operated, spoke, and reacted as if it were alive, with a continuous field of thought. It suddenly occurred to Ivan that the complexity of its system must be in a sense responsible for the development of a form of robotic consciousness that gives the impression that one is speaking to a living being, an entity in its own right, able to indulge in the most complex of discussions.

"Very well," said the robot rising from the chair. "Before we start the session, you will have the chance to relax a little. We here at the Philosophical Society know that our visitors have many deep questions to ask us. The best way for them to prepare is to relax a little. We place emphasis on psychological release. It helps our visitors better prepare for the session. So please, feel free to drink a little wine and eat ripe fruit. In my temporary absence you can enjoy the company of one of our hostesses, a lovely lady, just for a short time. It's all part of the session."

The robot left through a large, grey-coloured door. Ivan was completely unprepared for this unusual yet effective way of preparing one for a deep exchange. The robots certainly knew how to treat their visitors. The door opened again and this time a beautiful woman stepped in.

"Greetings Ivan... my name is Alicia."

She was bare foot, feet like well-sculptured marble. However, her right foot had an extra small toe, a mutation. Ivan spotted it but he was overwhelmed by her beauty as he regarded her. To him even the extra small toe was something to be admired. She was petite, dressed in a blue-white robe that matched her eyes, hair as black as ebony, skin pale white. Her face was chiselled to perfection, small nose, voluptuous lips and high cheek bones and yet there was something different about her, almost Earthly, something that the citizens of Mars lacked... her eyes and motion so distinct. She sat beside him...

"Tell me," he asked, "Were you born on Mars?"

"Yes. I was, in the city of New Beijing..."

"You just seem so different. I can't pinpoint it."

"Oh, I get that all the time. It's because I spent five Earth years living on the blue planet. I managed to get a work-visa, wanted a new experience."

"That's it... I knew there was something different about you. I've often wondered myself what it must be like there. Don't get me wrong, I'm quite well informed. Between the Martian media, and the tele-set I've learnt bits about the planet, the planet of our ancestors, without ever going there, but one still lacks a certain knowledge if one does not experience the real thing. Many speak fondly of it..."

She smiled, dimples forming and said, "It's so beautiful... so much to see. However, it did take me some time to adjust to the heavier gravity there, but I managed to adapt quite quickly."

"Tell me, many speak about the Amazon rainforest, its beauty."

"Ah," she muttered softly. "I went there. It was a real adventure like no other. For any Martian citizen it really is an experience not to be missed."

Her eyes now became distant and reflective. "The Amazon rainforest is a jungle with unparalleled biodiversity. The region is home to around 2.5 million insect species, tens of thousands of plants, and some 2,000 birds and mammals. The creatures that dwell there are quite unique, unlike anything you could imagine. To date, at least 40,000 plant species, 2,200 fishes, 427 mammals, 1,294 birds, 428 amphibians, and 378 reptiles have been scientifically classified in the region."

Ivan was taken aback by her vast knowledge. He said, "Such precise figures."

"I've studied much, plus I have a photographic memory." She smiled... a smile that lit up her chiselled face.

"Keep going," he said looking deeply into her eyes, almost hypnotized by her soft voice and beauty.

"Well... the jungle contains several species that can pose a hazard. Among the largest creatures are the black caiman, jaguar, and anaconda."

"Jaguar," he exclaimed with childish excitement. "Yes, I recall seeing one of those on a documentary. As for the others, I'm not too familiar but tell me about Earth's oceans. I have always found it somewhat amusing that a planet that is mostly made up of salt water should be named Earth. I mean how inappropriate to call a planet Earth when it is quite clearly mostly ocean."

"I see your point," she said with a tinkling chuckle that made Ivan melt a little. "Yes, about 71 percent of the Earth's surface is water-covered. I found that amusing myself." She paused then continued... "The inhabitants of Earth spend much of their time enjoying the sea... Swimming is a big thing there."

"Yes, I've heard this."

"To be honest, I could never find the courage to even place my toe in the sea never mind learn to swim. The seas of Earth are filled with all kinds of creatures, some extremely deadly. Ironically, my friends, the Earthlings I called them, found it rather amusing... but after what I learnt about the sea from them, I could never find the courage to go in, not even knee high. They all tried to persuade me, but I wouldn't budge."

"What exactly turned you away from such a unique experience Alicia?"

"There are many dangerous sea creatures... There's a very large fish known as Shark. Sharks are extremely dangerous, especially the White shark but also the Bull and Tiger. There are also many dangerous sea snakes. Snakes don't just live on land. Their distribution depends on the ocean temperatures, which depend on the amount of solar radiation reaching the surface. Ocean water contains large quantities of dissolved gases, including oxygen, carbon dioxide and nitrogen. This gas exchange takes place at the surface and solubility depends on the temperature and salinity of the water."

"Wow... you are one fine lady Alicia, very smart. Your time on Earth served you well..."

"Yes, it did, in more ways than one." She paused her eyes suddenly became distant and reflective. "It triggered a spiritual reaction within me. I started to gravitate towards theological and philosophical thought after my experience there. Earth is so very special Ivan. As I say it thrives with all kinds of complex life forms both on land and the sea... something that Mars is devoid of. This fabricated world of ours is nothing in comparison. But there, I'm probably boring you now."

"Please continue, I could listen to you all day," encouraged Ivan, his dark brown eyes deeply focused and intrigued.

"Well, to summarise, my time there catapulted me into a particular sphere of thought. To have been part of the earthly existence opened up a whole new way of thinking about life, the universe, and more importantly our place in it. As a result of what I experienced on that planet I am now a strong believer in God."

Ivan was completely captivated by what she had just said. He asked, "Are Earth people believers?"

"There are many but like here on Mars the people of Earth have mixed views... I guess that mankind, as a whole, has always had a tendency to view life through the grid of their mind-set. These are some

of the philosophies that many embrace not only on
Earth but here on Mars as I'm sure you know only
too well... Atheism, God doesn't exist. Agnosticism,
not sure. Pantheism, all is God. Monism, matter
and spirit are one. Mysticism, only spirit is real.
Materialism, only matter is real. Deism, creator can't
control. Humanism, man is God. Existentialism,
experience is God. Rationalism, reason is God.
Animism, spirits are gods. Polytheism, many gods.
Dualism, two gods, bad and good."

"That's quite a list, and yes I'm familiar with all
those."

"For sure," said Alicia smiling, "but, none of those
philosophies hold for me. As far as I'm concerned
God exists, one supreme, all-powerful God who is
in control of the universe, and all the mechanisms
of life. He must be eternal, creative, orderly... The
symmetry and mathematics of the universe would
suggest this. The complexity of life demands a
creator. For example, on planet Earth microscopic
bacteria preceded man by many thousands of years
in making a rotary engine. One type of bacterium
has hair-like extensions twisted together to form a
stiff spiral. It spins this corkscrew around like the
propeller of a ship and drives itself forward. It can
even reverse its engine." She smiled at the thought.
"Take the octopus and squid... Are you familiar?"

"Yes, I've come across them in many documentaries concerning Earth's oceans."

"Well, they suck water into a special chamber and then, with powerful muscles, expel it... This propels them forward - Jet propulsion... And Fish diffuse gas into or out of their swim bladders, altering buoyancy. All chance...? No, God has to be behind all life...."

"So, I guess that's what attracted you to come and work here at the Philosophical Society?"

"Yes, the Philosophical Society was the ideal place for me. Not to mention that all the robots here are theists too."

"I didn't realise that..." he confessed, a little surprised.

"You'll soon see." She winked. "Tell me Ivan, are you a theist?"

"As a matter of fact, I am..."

"Great."

"How long have you worked here?"

"Three years and I'm well-paid to entertain visitors like you with my humble presence."

"Yes, your beautiful presence."

She smiled bashfully. "By the way, I'm not the only woman working here in this capacity. There are another three, Ruth, Elaine and Jessie."

Ivan had lost all sense of time and the thirty minutes they had been talking flew past in a flash. As they sat there chatting away in the grand room, a certain bond had formed, a deep affinity... magnetic personalities the cause. Then looking deeply into her eyes, he suddenly wondered what she thought about the government, the so-called elite minds that were about to ironically steal the minds of all Martian citizens including Alicia's. *'Given her strong spiritual beliefs she has to be against it,'* he thought.

He leant closer to her, his voice soft, "Alicia what are your thoughts on the new law, the brain implants, mind-control?"

"Obviously I'm dead against it. It's the ultimate mind-invasion. I think anyone with a rational mind would be against the idea," she replied with a disgusted shake of her head.

"Yes, but so many Martian citizens seem to accept it as if it will benefit them... The Governing Leaders, headed by that man Roger J. Locke, the Supreme Leader, have used the media to brainwash the masses, and have presented the nano-chip as something almost divine. They have convinced them that this is the best way forward for the citizens of Mars. They say it will decrease crime and even prevent it but that will be at the expense of losing our souls! Sadly, the masses seem to have blindly accepted it. And when I say masses, I mean the majority of people. So, that logically implies that there is a corresponding minority against. People like you and I."

Alicia's eyes were wide and sad. "I have a friend that strongly opposes the new law. He would love to meet someone like you. He's not the kind of person you meet every day."

She pulled out a card from her robe. Printed across it was a number.

"Call me," she said, with a mysterious look in her eyes suggesting there was much more to discover.

Ivan took the card, examined it, and placed it in the inner pocket of his grey coat. He was intrigued.

Without prolonging the discussion any further he said, "I will call you; you can count on that. I would love to meet this person."

The silence that fell between them was interrupted when the door opened and the robot returned.

"Thank you, Alicia, that will be all."

She looked at Ivan holding his gaze a moment too long and said, "It was nice meeting you." He watched her as she walked to the door and stepped out.

"I trust you found Alicia entertaining..." The robot's soft voice brought him back to the reason he had come.

"Yes, she's a terrific lady, very engaging and highly intelligent."

"Yes, indeed. We prize such qualities here at the Philosophical Society," said the robot Alexis sitting on a chair. "So, tell me, how would you like to start our meeting, what would you like to know?"

Rubbing his eyes Ivan replied, "Well I guess I have many questions to ask."

"I see you brought a book with you." It pointed at the volume Ivan had placed on the table. "Books these days are scarce, especially here on Mars. Why did you bring it?"

"Cab rides tend to be boring, and I enjoy the tactility of the genuine article. It's a science-history book. I'm fascinated with the history of Mars and how our ancestors got here, and the terraforming process involved. I spent yesterday morning watching a great documentary concerning these matters."

"So, what would you like to know?"

"Okay Alexis, I guess I'll just fire my questions out in random order if that's okay?" The robot inclined its head in affirmation. With mind-control firmly on his mind but not wanting to go into the subject with a robot, Ivan calculatingly asked, "What is thought? Please answer from the perspective of a human being."

"Now that's a wonderful question to ask a robot Ivan. And one that bares great significance given what is happening at present."

Ivan looked away briefly, slightly embarrassed. He should have known the robot would see through his question.

Seconds of silence past and he wondered if it was going to answer. It bent its head looking at the floor as if saddened and said, "I am aware of the new law Ivan, a diabolical law that threatens the souls of all the people of Mars. All the citizens of the Martian world will soon have their thoughts monitored. I am deeply saddened, but unfortunately nothing can be done to stop it. We at the Philosophical Society are strongly against it... you have our sympathies."

Ivan had not expected such a reaction. He was struck hard by its words. It was kind of ironic that a programmed machine would say such a thing, he thought.

The robot looked back up and said, "Now Ivan, in answer to your question... Thoughts are energy signals. The energy transmitting a thought therefore has mass. The ions and molecules encoding the energetic signal have mass too."

"I bet those damn government leaders can't wait to calculate the weight of my thoughts," Ivan interjected, "Calculating the weight of a single thought... well I'm sure that they are more than able given what they are doing."

The robot responded, "In terms of weight, it will certainly be an infinitesimally tiny number, but not zero."

Ivan's face clouded in reddish anger as he thought of the implications. He composed himself...

"I'm sorry Ivan but you brought up the subject," apologised the robot, then continued...

"Moving on, a thought is a representation of something. A representation is a likeness, a thing that depicts another thing by having characteristics that correspond to that other thing. A map is another example of a representation. If you like, the mind is a kind of map. The brain and the mind, evolved as a map of the body's relation to its external environment. Fundamentally, thoughts are maps representing and corresponding to things that people's brains have either perceived with their senses, felt with their emotions, or formed as an action plan. All of these are electrochemically mediated processes. Thoughts may be fleeting, or they may later be consolidated as memories. Memory too is a physical process, encoded by structural molecular changes in neuronal connections.

Now... let's consider how sensory perceptions are transduced by the sense organs into neural signals. Imagine hearing a loud noise that surprises and frightens you. The sound of the loud noise is transformed from a specific pattern of sound waves in the air to a corresponding pattern of vibrations transmitted through your eardrum and the small bones in your middle ear to your cochlea, then to a corresponding pattern of electrochemical impulses along the auditory nerve, to corresponding signals in neurons in the auditory cortex and association cortex. It also activates fear circuitry, relayed via the Amygdala and perhaps also visual circuitry that records what you saw at that moment. These signals are transmitted between neurons by chemical neurotransmitters. The entire widely distributed network activated throughout the cerebral cortex by this stimulus is the experience at that moment. Since this was such a strong stimulus the pattern of connections in this particular network is then made permanently retrievable. This happens by changes in membrane proteins at the connections between all the participating neurons that fired together in response to that stimulus... in other words neurons that fire together, wire together. This constitutes the memory. The same approximate network can be reactivated in the future by a reminder. The pattern of connections is a representation, a map, corresponding to the pattern of information that you perceived. Now complex information such as memory is distributed. The memory of, let's say your grandfather, is not contained in one neuron. There is a vast network of often distant neurons that, in their connections with each other, collectively represent the grandfather memory. Moving on... the conscious sense of self emerges from loops of self-referent symbolic representations. The psychological self emerges from abstract feedback loops of self-referent symbolic representations, recursively reflecting on itself in a reverberating circuit."

Ivan sat there absorbed. "That's a lot of information Alexis."

"Yes Ivan, we pride ourselves on this. In summary, the symbiotic connection of neurons in your brain sparks thought process. Now when it comes down to machines, like me, it's all to do with mathematical algorithms bits of programming logic that govern the mathematical pathways of a robotic mind. In times past, Earthly man studied cognitive psychology, how humans think, and they attempted to write mathematical formulas... algorithms, that mimic the logical mechanisms of human intelligence, and this was achieved with mind-blowing results." It smiled as it self-reflected. "The cells of the nervous system Ivan are the closest thing in the universe to the transistors and gates of a computer. In short, a biological brain is the closest thing to a computer, regardless of the different processes involved."

It paused then continued...

"These algorithms, bits of programming logic, instruct us machines how to act and be, and as you can see, it works remarkably well. It allows us robots to identify related concepts and make the kind of intuitive connections we call experience. Probability is a massive component of higher-level machine reasoning, using unprecedented processing power to give the most likely answer from a virtually limitless range of knowledge. Robots are brilliant statisticians, and with the right algorithms, we can quickly make billions of calculations to decide which answer or action is most likely to produce the desired result. We make decisions based on evidence and probability. This is due to mathematical models which in turn create logical processes. Computer programming languages are grounded in logic. But it goes so much deeper than all of this. Ultimately, all thought, whether human or machine, no matter how induced is connected to the eternal source, a being that transcends time and space and dwells in eternity."

"A theistic robot... interesting," said Ivan, curious. "I already knew. Alicia told me."

"We machines at the Philosophical Society are all theists, how could we not be? And you Ivan?"

"Yes, I certainly believe in a higher power, that's for sure."

"That's rare on Mars. Many of the Martian citizens that come here are acute atheists. But many leave completely changed after the session. They see the light of theism and are drawn into that theological sphere."

Seconds of silence fell...

"One of the robots here along with me specialises in theological philosophy, its name is Clarence. We argue that the mind and brain are separate. The mind is the soul of man, a nexus of electromagnetic forces, the spiritual dimension of the person, nonphysical. The brain in turn is a physical machine, an electrochemical organ, it has weight and dimension and is made up of hundreds of different structures each working symbiotically. All thought starts off as nonphysical in the mind, but once channelled into the brain via the mind, it then becomes a physical process, these energy signals."

"Makes sense to me."

"We also argue that man is indeed free, made in the image of God and that determinism ultimately holds no truth because the mind is separate from the brain, and God has ultimately given man total freedom regardless of the brain being a biological machine."

"Please explain more Alexis," urged Ivan as it paused again.

"Well, the brain, as a biological machine is bound by the laws of science. It simply has to obey certain laws of biology, chemistry, physics and so forth. Breaking it down further, the brain is made up of quantum fields, subatomic particles that behave in a particular way, thus one could come to the conclusion that free will is ultimately an illusion because the brain is a machine that fundamentally obeys and is bound by the laws of quantum mechanics. It is subject to electrical and chemical activity, hormonal activity that ultimately shapes Man's choices, desires, and decisions. Thus, freedom of choice, free will, many believe today is nothing but an illusion. But when you consider that the mind is separate from the brain and that all decision making takes place there in the nonphysical mind, then man is indeed free, regardless of the symbiotic association between mind and brain. In essence the brain only operates as a receiver."

Silence fell... both man and machine thinking...

"There is however a scientist here on Mars, a professor of biology who is an atheist, Don A. Heinlein. He argues that there is no free will. We at the Philosophical Society all disagree with him for the reasons I've given... God has blessed mankind with free will. Not to mention that if human beings both on Earth and here on Mars believe that there is no free will it would surely cause existential despair. In other words what Heinlein is preaching is dangerous, soul destroying with deep existential and psychological implications. How does man avoid complete existential despair if he believes that he is just a biological machine obeying the same laws of the physical universe as any other thing made up of atoms? How does a human avoid the existential despair of... what is this all for, I'm not free, thus life is ultimately pointless? How is mankind supposed to go about everyday life if anything they feel entitled to isn't ultimately true... if there's no such thing as appropriate blame or punishment or praise or reward? I find it an incredibly daunting task to calculate how a human being is supposed to live life thinking that way. If there is no free will, one can't be blamed, one can't be praised. Human beings are just following biological luck. Regardless, this is all hypothetical. This atheistic professor is preaching nonsense. As I have already mentioned... man is free to choose, blessed by the will of God, made in the image of the eternal God."

"This is fascinating Alexis. How does Heinlein justify his argument?"

"I will quote from one of his lectures."

'Man is not free... Man does not have a shred of free will, none at all. Free will is a complete, utter, illusion. The reason for this is... you behave, you make a choice, and to understand why you did that and where that intention came from, well part of it was due to the sensory environment you were in a minute ago. We are constantly buffered and swayed by sensory information that seems irrelevant and hardly noticeable as well as by sensory information that is entirely subliminal. Now, some of it is from the hormone levels in your bloodstream that morning, and some of it is from whether you had a good or stressful last four months and what sort of neuroplasticity has occurred with your brain. Furthermore, part of it is what hormone levels you were exposed to as a fetus as bizarre as that might sound. All of these are relevant factors that ultimately melt into one major factor. Now if you're talking about what evolution, that highly complex convoluted process has to do with your behavior, you are talking about genetics. If you are talking about what your genes have to do with behavior, you are talking about how your brain was constructed or what proteins are coded for. They are all intertwined, all inter-connected. And when you look at all those influences, basically, the challenge is… show me a neuron that just caused that behavior or show me a network of neurons that just caused that behavior and show me that nothing about what they just did was influenced by anything from the sensory environment one second ago to the evolution of your species.'

Ivan interjected. "That's quite a statement Alexis."

"Yes, but of course he is fundamentally wrong, God makes all the difference as I have explained, man is free in Him, not to mention that the mind is separate to the brain."

"Does he say anything else about this?"

"Yes. He goes on to say in his lecture, word for word, the following…"

'There simply is no free will. For example… show me the free neuron? Let's say you perform an action, a task, a basic one… Neurobiologists can go and find the neuron in your motor cortex which sent the signal to those muscles to flex, and you could find the neurons in what are called the pre-motor cortex which sent signals which triggered that motor cortex to send that signal… and, you could then find neurons in the frontal cortex that triggered that… and find neurons in the prefrontal cortex that triggered that… and neurons in emotional parts of the brain that triggered those neurons. Now show me the neuron that started that cascade… a neuron that fired that had an action potential for no reason whatsoever, a neuron whose firing was not regulated by the physical laws of the universe that happened for no prior causal antecedent reason. Show me a neuron that started that… and that works that way, and then, only then we could talk about free will.

Now let's look at quantum mechanics. Quantum mechanics is the branch of physics that deals with the behavior of matter and light on a subatomic and atomic level… It attempts to explain the properties of atoms and molecules and their fundamental particles like protons, neutrons, electrons, gluons, and quarks… quantum entanglement, non-locality over space and time, quantum tunneling, wave-particle duality. These are all the things that are occurring at a subatomic level. Now if that's going to have anything to do with why you are a kind, sweet person, or why you were selfish and evil, those quantum effects are going to have to bubble up 20-30 orders of magnitude to begin to explain a single action potential which takes about 3-4 milliseconds. That is about 10 to the 23rd times longer in duration than a quantum effect… That's a heck of a lot of bubbling up you need to do to get to just that level of biology. You simply cannot get the bubbling up even if a quantal effect in this one synapse has synchronized through superposition and quantum entanglement and has entangled the events of 4000 other synapses. You're using about a trillion synapses, emptying about a trillion axon terminals full of neurotransmitter, every time you do an action… There's very little evidence that it bubbles up. The second huge problem is… even if it did bubble up that high, the colossal problem is quantum indeterminacy cannot be the explanation for free will…'

Again, Ivan interjected… "This professor is extremely intelligent but as you mentioned his problem is that he is an atheist looking and analyzing this great philosophical question from an atheistic perspective."

"Yes Ivan, that's right…"

"Please continue… I'm intrigued to hear the rest of his argument however wrong, he maybe."

"Certainly… In his lecture he goes on to say the following…"

'It is absolutely impossible to make sense of anything that we think, do, feel, or remember, out of the context of the neurobiology that went on one second ago. And the environmental triggers of that neurobiology that went on one minute ago and the neural plasticity over recent months, and your adolescence, and your childhood, and the epigenetics of your fetal life and your genes, and the culture that your ancestors came up with, and the ecosystems that made those cultures, and millions of years of evolution and so forth. In short, all we are is the sum of what our biology and its interactions with the environment have been. We are the sum of all of those biological factors that have made us who we are in this instance. We are the outcomes of the sheer random, good and bad biological luck that each of us has stumbled into… There is nothing in the biology of our behavior that just happens from out of nowhere. Every single biological event that we have has a history. Every bit of behavior has multiple levels of causality, and so forth.

However, one important thing to note here is organisms do change. Change can happen. We do not choose to change because we do not choose to do anything because we can't, because there is no free will. We are a mechanistic biological machine that is not free. We are changed by circumstance. Furthermore, change can happen within a framework of a mechanistic neurobiology. Not only can prenatal hormone exposure change the way your brain is being constructed, but learning that prenatal hormone exposure can change the construction of your brain will change your brain right now, and how you think about where your intentions came from… The knowledge of the knowledge is an effector in and of itself. Neurons grow new processes, circuits disconnect… Everything in the brain indeed changes and out of this, come extraordinary examples of human change.'

"Okay Ivan, I will stop here. I think I have given you enough."

Ivan rubbed his jaw. "Wow… that's some argument. No matter how wrong he is, he certainly knows his stuff."

"Yes, an intelligent man who is sadly blinded by atheism. With God in the equation Ivan, looking into that deep theological reality, everything changes regardless of what he said, however technical and seemingly plausible. You are ultimately free because of Him, the eternal source that made you that way and indeed all Man both on Earth and Mars."

Moments of silence passed while Ivan absorbed what he had just learned.

"Okay, well, tell me," he said, eventually, hungry for more. "Away from this, in the context of a human being, could consciousness arise out of electromagnetic fields? And please feel free to drift into other areas of science which correlate."

"Light photon energy is continuously transforming potential energy into the kinetic energy of matter, in the form of electrons. Kinetic energy is the energy of what is actually happening. This emergent electromagnetic activity would be fundamental to how the brain produces consciousness in a similar way to how electromagnetic waves are fundamental to how a radio produces music. The fact that light has momentum and momentum is frame dependent could give us a physical reason why conscious awareness is always in the centre of its own reference frame, in 'the moment of now' being able to look back in time in all directions at the beauty of the stars. Conscious awareness is the most advanced part of a universal process and is an integral part of the dynamic structure of the universe. The Universe is a continuum with the future coming into existence photon by photon with each new photon electron coupling. This forms the movement of positive and negative charge with the continuous flow of electromagnetic fields. Consciousness in the form of electrical activity in the brain is the most advanced part of this process and can therefore comprehend this process as 'time,' with a past that has gone forever and a future that is always uncertain in the form of a probability function or quantum wave particle function. Therefore, every individual is in the centre of their own reference frame as an interactive part of this process being able to look back in time in all directions at the beauty of the stars. It is this personalisation of the brain being in 'the moment of now' in the centre of its own reference frame that gives people the concept of 'mind' with each one having their own personal view of the beauty and uncertainty of life.

Additionally, the arrow of Time is formed by the quantum wave particle function with the future continuously coming into existence with each new photon electron coupling or dipole moment. The photon of quantum mechanics forms the movement of electromagnetic fields. Time is continuously being formed by the spontaneous absorption and emission of light waves. Atoms are forming their own future relative to their energy and momentum. Water molecules will do this by continuously forming and breaking hydrogen bonds relative to the flow of the water. The molecules of water are constantly moving in relation to each other, and the hydrogen bonds are continually breaking and reforming. This process forms dipole moments with the separation of charge with the absorption and emission of photo energy. This represents the future coming into existence photon by photon within the reference frame of the water relative to the energy and momentum of the water molecules.

Furthermore, the flow of Time as a process of continuous energy exchange, change and your consciousness as a stream of unbroken ever-changing flow of ideas, feelings, perceptions, and emotions are interlinked. You have electrical activity relative to the structure of the brain forming chemical changes or chemical reactions. Chemical energy is stored in the bonds that hold the atoms together. When the bonds form and break you have the continuous exchange of photon energy with the future unfolding relative to the electrical activity and the structure of the brain. Finally, Space and Time are properties of quanta or photon energy. This process forms the ever-changing world of your everyday life. You have a unique and uncertain future unfolding at the smallest unit of energy with each new photon oscillation or vibration. Each photon electron coupling, or dipole moment, only occurs once, but the process of energy exchange forms the movement of positive and negative charge..."

Silence fell as again Ivan took a moment for his brain to catch up. The robot was an awesome repository of information.

Ivan said, "That's some explanation. I've always been deeply fascinated by the structure of existence."

"It's actually rather simple. If you want to know the secrets of the universe, think in terms of energy, frequency, and vibration... resonance. E=mc2 can be rewritten as... energy is to mass as space2 is to time2. In this universe of Mass, Energy, Space, and Time: Space and Time are the field of action. Every object in the field consists of both Mass and Energy together, in all cases, even though only observed as one or the other, ever. All things exist as a dichotomy of Mass and Energy in a continuum of Space and Time. Existence is mass, energy, motion, in space time. The speed of light is just a finite limit. Things exist at speeds slower than light and all different mass to energy ratios. Mass/Energy objects exist as particles or waves that move through the field of space and time that they create in their energy/mass relationships.

Different kinds of particles move through both space and time at different rates of space per time. The minimums of both motions are one Planck Space and one Planck Time. This is the speed of light and other 0 mass Bosons. At speeds slower than light, are the inertial mass Fermions that cannot go as fast as light without infinite energy. At low energies, Fermions are virtually still, relative to each other. Particles that are faster than light are the Tachyons with imaginary mass that approach infinite speed at low energies. It takes infinite energy to slow Tachyons down to the speed of light. A Tachyon is received before it is emitted. It is pre-causal. The three axes of Space are mutually perpendicular. Three planes intersect at a cubic point. Simple local flat stackable cubic space is defined by three mutually perpendicular pairs of parallel planes. The diagonals of the facets on a cube form a set of dual tetrahedrons. There are actually three axes of time, just like space, but they are parallel to each other, not perpendicular... they flow along together. Events, like the existence of objects, occur in the past, the present, and the future. All waves, all objects in the present, resonate with each other to exist, as standing waves. The resonant energy of objects can reflect upon the past, and project into the future. Resonating in the dynamic and constantly changing present is the event of being. Existence is participatory. All things resonate with all other things. Being is change. Being is having a resonant interface with all other things in the here and now, which is in motion, and processing those changes in space and time. No change means, no existence in the present. All things have the ultimate goal of continuing to be. To be, is to resonate...

Four-Dimensional Space/Time, viewed from a perspective of changes in three dimensions, is like passing a two-dimensional plane through a three-dimensional object. You may see a different resonant symmetry, depending on perspective. Perspectives on reality can differ, and still be valid... With motion, and constant change in perspective, there will be constant change in the resonant interactions between things. Changes between resonators, creates disharmony, dissonance and discord. Resonators adapt by exchanging tensions in quantitative incremental intervals of change in spacing and timing. Perspective dictates patterns of resonance.

Resonant waves exist in exact numbers of waves per space. Thus... we are forced to conclude that energy is gained or lost in discrete units, like changes in waves per space. Energy emissions in the electron shells of an atom proceed along understood intervals of resonant stability. Greater intervals can skip lesser intermediate energy levels. Atoms emit all excess energy down to their base vibration. In a sun, fusing hydrogen emits energy as protons and neutrons join up. There are different pathways of possible sequences to achieve stable two proton two neutron helium, with known probabilities for each path. Space and time have rational values for all points in space/time. Changes will be from one rational value to another rational value; from one fraction to another fraction, which resonate in their common denominators. Objects manage energy through harmonic resonant interval units of change for resolution from tension. Entities harmonize 'musically' to resonate their being and have a perspective on all other resonant structures. Resonant interaction is the music of being of each thing with all other things. Resonance is a standing wave, which can be straight or curved. Two standing waves can be parallel or perpendicular. Perpendicular waves can be in phase or out of phase. When two perpendicular waves are in phase, the intersection is a straight diagonal line. When two waves are out of phase, the intersection is a circle... All mass/energy entities exist as self-reflecting standing waves, which appear to flow and resonate in two contradictory directions at the same time. Any entity is a bi-stable image of change. Resonant harmonic standing waves exist in discrete divisions of the field of opposing tensions that those waves exist and propagate in. These standing waves all exist in the same space and time and resonate with each other through all their mutual rational fractions of time and space.

Lastly, objectivity and subjectivity are equally important in the structure of existence, but different.

Objectively all things or events are different from all other things, yet all perspectives or viewpoints share the same pervasive, repeatable, physical reality. Subjectively, all things or events are similar to all other things, in innumerable ways. Yet every entity has its own unique subjective reality..."

There was another pause. Ivan knew it would take him weeks of reflection to assimilate all he was hearing but he wanted more...

"Okay Alexis, moving on... A more specific question... Our actions in the past are correlated to our experience of the future. But a growing number of scientists are convinced the future influences the past. Thus, what if this forward causality could somehow be reversed in time allowing actions in the future to influence outcomes in the past? What are your thoughts?"

The robot's refined metal face now seemed to glow with an almost organic eloquence, as if it had transmuted from an inanimate machine into a living being. It said, "Well Ivan, this mind-bending notion is retrocausality and it is a deep subject. Even though it may feel verboten to consider a future that affects the past, it could account for some of the strange phenomena observed in quantum physics, which exists on the tiny scale of atoms. But the renewed curiosity about retrocausality is driven by more recent findings about quantum mechanics. Unlike the familiar macroscopic world that we inhabit governed by classical physics, the quantum world allows for inexplicably seemingly bizarre phenomena. Now particles at these scales can pierce right through seemingly impassable barriers, quantum tunnelling. Furthermore, these particles can occupy many different states simultaneously. This is known as superposition. The properties of quantum objects can also somehow become synced together even if they are located light years apart... quantum entanglement. Now Retrocausal models open avenues of exploring a 'time-symmetric' view of our universe, in which the laws of physics are the same regardless of whether time runs forward or backward. In any model where you had an event in the past correlated with your future choice of setting, that would be Retrocausal. If you think things should be time-symmetric, there's an argument to be made that you need some retrocausality to make sense of quantum mechanics in a time-symmetric way."

It paused in thought, calculating, then continued...

"It's important to emphasize that retrocausality is not the same as time travel. These models don't predict that signals or objects... including human beings... could be dispatched to the past, in part because there is no evidence that we are currently being deluged with any such future messages, or messengers. You have to be very careful in a retrocausal model because the fact of the matter is we can't send signals back in time. It's important that we can't, because if we could, then we could produce all sorts of vehicles or paradoxes. You have to make sure your model doesn't allow that. Instead, retrocausal models suggest that there is a mechanism that allows circumstances in the future to correlate with past states."

"I see," said Ivan softly. Although fully gripped by what he was hearing, his mind was now swaying back towards the mind-control problem at hand. His mind was split...

The robot continued... "Another possible big payoff is that retrocausality supports the so-called 'epistemic' view of the wave function in the usual quantum mechanics description... the idea that it is just an encoding of our incomplete knowledge of the system. That makes it much easier to understand the so-called collapse of the wave function, as a change in information..."

"This is all so fascinating and highly complex. I could listen to you all day, but time is limited unfortunately. Could we jump ahead into new territory...? Tell me, does anything await a robot beyond... let's use the words 'mechanical death.' When you cease to be, what will happen?"

"Well Ivan, let me answer your question like this... when Man dies, he will stand before God. He will either spend the rest of eternity with God or be separated from Him. God will judge Man's heart. There are moral and ethical implications attached. Now robots like me, machines have an expiry date. Beyond that we cease to exist. Thus, we do not have the capacity to live on because we lack a soul, a spirit, regardless of how alive we seem. To be truly alive means to be human. Man is comprised of body, soul and spirit. You are eternal. Life, your existence here, is just an illusion compared with what lies beyond."

Ivan felt profoundly saddened by what the robot had just said. It was hard to consider that such a wonderful entity would just cease to exist one day.

"Now let me add this," continued Alexis, "in a sense man is a triune being made up of body, that is the carnal, soul, that is the mind, will, emotions and the spirit which is the essence of who you truly are. Interestingly, the universe itself can be looked at as a trinity. It is comprised of space, time, and matter. It's a space-time-matter continuum. Space is three dimensional, and within each dimension it permeates all space. The reality of any portion of space is obtained by multiplying the three dimensions together... 1x1x1=1.

Now Time itself can also be considered as triune... past, present and potential future. In turn the three create the totality of time. Lastly Matter, and when I say Matter, I am referring to light and sound. Thus, Matter is unseen omnipresent Energy manifesting itself in various forms of measurable motion, then experienced in corresponding phenomena... light and sound. Now light energy generates light waves, which are experienced in the seeing of light. Sound energy generates sound waves which we experience when we hear sound. Thus, Ivan, the physical universe itself can be logically seen as a triune universe."

"Fascinating," muttered Ivan... "Okay Alexis, but can you define God?"

"God is a spirit. He is eternal. He dwells outside the sphere of time and space. He is not bound by time. He can see the past, present and future in an instant. The eternality of God transcends science and human understanding. God is..."

Ivan was not sure he really absorbed the last thirty minutes of his session properly. It was truly enlightening, and he resolved to book another session with Alexis as soon as he could. He had certainly enjoyed his time at the Philosophical Society and Alexis the robot had delivered beyond expectation.

It had been a great education, so deep and intriguing and it had given him some peace considering his fears over the situation at hand.

Late that night, back at his hut with the lights lowered to dim he was deep in thought, going through all he had learned when, all of a sudden, he remembered Alicia and the friend she had spoken of who opposed the new law. He recalled her words, 'He would love to meet someone like you. He's not the kind of person you meet every day.' His inner senses told him that this was the man who could potentially offer a solution to the problem. Given the circumstances and the power held by the Governing Leaders, it would have to be a miracle solution. He roused himself from his introspection and rose to his feet, removed the card from his jacket that lay on the sofa and studied the number. Moving toward the tele-set-screen he dialled. The line buzzed as the circuit was established. Alicia's face appeared across the screen.

"Ivan it's you!" exclaimed Alicia. She seemed to be genuinely pleased he had called.

"Yes," he said. "Did you doubt it?"

She smiled... "It's seldom that I bond to someone so quickly. It's as if I have known you all my life."

"I know what you mean." He paused as he searched for words. "Look Alicia, this friend of yours, I would like to meet him as soon as possible."

She interjected... "Ivan I have already spoken to him about you... told him everything. As soon as I got home, I called. He's ready to see you anytime. He can't wait."

"Great, how about tomorrow, say 9:30pm."

"Perfect... the later the better. I will let him know. I will see you there."

Ivan now thought about his friend Orson. He said, "Alicia I would like to bring a friend. He's a very close friend. We think alike, if you know what I mean..."

"That's absolutely fine... This is the address." She began to type briskly. The address was then displayed across the tele-set-screen. He made a note...

"Got it... I will be there tomorrow 9:30pm with my friend. See you there Alicia. You will be there?"

She smiled her eyes warm and inviting. "Yes Ivan, I will be there. Goodnight."

He grinned and then disconnected. Then he dialled again, this time Orson. His friend's face looked tired as it appeared across the screen in ripples of visual static.

"Ivan, everything okay?" Orson asked between yawns. "How did your meeting go at the Philosophical Society?"

"It went better than I could have ever expected. In fact, so well, that tomorrow night I'm meeting someone, this someone is anti-government, anti-nano-chip."

"And...?"

"Look, no time for details. I will pick you up tomorrow night around 8:40 pm. I'll explain everything then."

"This sounds a little fishy to me, but okay, I trust you. See you then..."

Ivan cut the line. He walked over to the multi-coloured sofa and sat. Tomorrow was all set. It was now time to relax and disconnect if that was possible. Picking up the glittering silver remote he flicked through the channels. He found something of interest and raised the volume. It was a documentary about the Gobi Desert on planet Earth. The show was titled: The Wonders of Earth. Images appeared. *'It resembled Mars prior to being terraformed,'* he thought. The narrator spoke as pictures flashed across the screen.

"The Gobi Desert which is found on Planet Earth is a vast, arid region spanning parts of northern China and southern Mongolia. It is known for its dunes, mountains and rare animals such as snow leopards and Bactrian camels. The combined effects of mountain building, the mid-latitude, westerly circulation and changes in the Asian monsoon, accompanied by global cooling, were principally responsible for the formation of modern Gobi Desert landscapes in central and eastern Asia during the late Pliocene. This desert occupies a vast arc of land 1,000 miles long and 300 to 600 miles wide, with an estimated area of 500,000 square miles. Its plains consist of chalk and other sedimentary rocks that are chiefly Cenozoic in age though some of the low, isolated hills are older. In the central Gobi the remains of dinosaurs from the Mesozoic Era and fossils of Cenozoic mammals have been found. The desert also contains Palaeolithic and Neolithic sites occupied by ancient people. Now, archaeologists and palaeontologists have done excavations in the Nemegt Basin in the north-western part of the Gobi Desert in Mongolia, which is noted for its fossil treasures, including early mammals, dinosaur eggs, and prehistoric stone implements."

He changed the channel... Another documentary. Ironically the face of Professor Don A. Heinlein appeared. He was being interviewed by a woman.

Ivan knew it was him because his name was imprinted across the screen.

Don A. Heinlein was saying, "Genetics, your genes, your DNA sequences, experience doesn't change those. What epigenetic experience changes though is the regulation of those genes when they are activated. We have early environment shaping all sorts of aspects of how the brain and the endocrine systems are put together, and most importantly, thanks to these epigenetic changes starting during fetal life environment does not begin at birth, these changes can be long-lasting, life-long, even multi-generational. Early environmental experience sculpts the construction of the brain and endocrine systems. This can involve epigenetic changes in gene regulation that can be life-long. Some of these acquired traits will influence the next generation's fetal environment…"

"Enough!" Ivan pleaded with the screen. He'd had his fill of this at the Philosophical Society. He changed the channel again. This time a young-looking black-haired scientist, Dietrich Bonhoeffer appeared on the screen and said, "A space elevator here on Mars would greatly improve Mars' exportation capabilities… Martian minerals, and so forth. Transportation from Mars' surface to Mars' orbit and vice versa can be achieved by a Space Elevator. The idea is to install a high-tensile rope from the surface to the synchronous orbit and a certain length beyond, connected to a counterweight. Since the gravity of Mars is lower than the gravity of Earth the requirements for the tensile strength of the rope is less, making this construction easier."

He paused as a diagram appeared behind him.

"Now the standard concept is for a system with a cabin, a climber, moving up or down a cable, the tether. The cable extends beyond the geostationary orbit to act as a counterweight to the cable. There is of course the moon problem to consider. The moons Phobos and Deimos are in low orbit and would intersect the cable in intervals. To deal with this situation an active adjustment of the cable's position might be required to avoid a collision. The Deimos problem might be solved by replacing the extension of the elevator by a counterweight located below Deimos' orbit. A non-equatorial space tether might allow for sufficient distance from the orbit of Phobos, if such an infrastructure can be built and put in place."

Ivan switched off the vision set and rubbed his eyes. He had heard about this countless times before. Many of the scientists on Mars constantly spoke about Phobos, and how this moon was an obstacle for building a space elevator. Had the moon been brought crashing down onto the surface of Mars in the early days during the terraforming project, when the planet was desolate, it would have benefited Mars greatly in so many ways including the terraforming project itself.

Ivan became aware that he was finally relaxing a little. '*My brainwaves are switching from alpha to theta, higher amplitude, lower frequency,*' he thought to himself, smiling as he realised, he had heard this in his mind in the voice of Alexis the robot. I need sleep... he decided and took himself off to bed.

It was a new day on Mars. Ivan spent most of it writing and working on some articles. As a journalist most of his writing was done at home. Occasionally he would be called into head office to meet with his superiors. He was one of the main columnists there. He had written many articles for the Martian chronicle, mostly things pertaining to Martian economics, and politics. '*Time for a break,*' he thought.

He rose from the chair, straightened out the kinks in his spine and made his way from his small office into the large kitchen. Across the wall was a large picture of planet Earth, underneath were the words, 'Equatorial Diameter: 7927 miles. Polar Diameter: 7900 miles. Oblateness: one 298th. Density: 5.41.'

Further along was a Martian 24-month calendar. One Martian year equated to two Earth years. The 24-month calendar had been well established. The forefathers were responsible for creating the calendar which alternated between familiar Earth months and the newly created ones.

He prepared some food and sat at the breakfast table to eat it. Three fried eggs with soft bread, was one of his favourite snacks. He was eating away when he heard someone call out.

"Fruit juices..." The voice was high pitched.

Once a week, the same man would come by, looking to sell Martian fruit juice. He would circle the area hoping for some business. This was common on Mars. The man's prices were reasonable, far cheaper than the main shopping centres. Ivan rose to his feet and somewhat reluctantly went to the front door. He saw the familiar large white truck.

"Hi, Mr Dobrovolski," said the man standing in the dim sunlight dressed in a one-piece light-blue Martian suit. He was almost too well dressed for such an occupation.

"Hi there Mr Larson..."

Larson walked over and halting beside Ivan, his green eyes dull with fatigue, enquired, "Anything this week?"

"Not this week my friend, I still have lots left over from last. But thank you anyway."

"No problem. I'm almost done for today... started real early. It's hard to make a living on Mars these days. Things have changed so much... so much so that I'd think about moving to Earth if I could, but even then, I would have to wait until all the citizens of Mars have had the implant, that nano-chip implant they're talking about. Travel is banned right now. And boy does that scare me, the thought of my brain being constantly surveyed."

Ivan sympathised. "Yes, I know exactly what you mean... Worrying times indeed..."

"Yes, very Mr Dobrovolski... and there's no escape. The Governing Leaders of Mars are nothing but tyrants. The Supreme Leader finally made the ultimate decision. Well to hell with him and the others I say. My brother's best friend has already been 'invited' for his implant. They're certainty not wasting any time with this."

A feeling of dread trickled down Ivan's spine. He knew that all the Martian citizens were doomed...

unless a miracle solution could be found. Tonight, he would discover if there was any such miracle. He seriously doubted it, after all what could be done? But he hoped.

"Well, I am sure glad that you see it that way Larson. Many of the citizens of Mars seem to be okay with it which concerns me greatly."

"Me too," said Mr Larson, "Good day to you sir!" As he walked back to his truck, he called over his shoulder, "We need a miracle, a saviour. Take care, Mr Dobrovolski."

Those words resonated with Ivan. A miracle, a saviour was indeed needed... But what were the chances? He turned and made his way back into the hut shutting out the noise of the truck driving slowly away.

The rest of the day passed in a bit of a blur but as darkness descended Ivan climbed out of his surface vehicle and made his way over to Lyons Snack-Bar. Martian citizens sat around eating and drinking, mouths flapping in idle discussion. On one side a group of mutants sat smoking and sipping at their strong beer. In the background Arabian music was playing faintly, yet clearly audible. How the citizens of Mars loved their music, especially the sounds that came from Earth. Again, he was struck by the fact that everyone seemed overly relaxed and calm, given what was happening to the planet. He made his way to a table and sat, waiting patiently for the waitress to come over. He checked his watch. It was 8pm. In forty minutes, he would meet Orson. From there they would make their way over to the unknown man's place, a twenty-minute ride. He had it all timed and Alicia would be there. He couldn't wait.

"Can I help you, Sir?" said the young brunette lady, slender and attractive. Her dimpled cheeks stood out, so too her blue eyes.

"A glass of Earth-imported white wine please."

Pulling out a small credit register from her loose-fitting green apron, she said, "Payment first I'm afraid. Sorry sir, it's just that we have had some problems with the locals in the past."

"No problem," he replied pulling out his silver-metallic card from his jacket. He fed it into the credit register. Credits taken...

The waitress moved away swiftly blending into the chaos of the bar... Ivan waited patiently until she returned with his glass of wine. He sipped at it, gazing absently at the bustling waitresses, everything passing in a blur. Then he noticed two well-dressed men looking over at him coldly. Why were they looking? Were they government spies? Had they monitored his discussions? Bugs were frequently used by the government. Calls were frequently monitored. Was he being paranoid? He turned his face away from them looking down at the table, wondering. Perhaps it was just him misinterpreting things. Regardless, the warm cosy atmosphere now began to dissolve. He felt weighed down by tension, cold and alone. He gulped the rest of his wine and made his way out, studiously ignoring the two men. Reaching his surface vehicle, he opened the door and sat, composing himself and then minutes later he was on his way. He drove past the police headquarters. *'They will soon be out of business,'* he thought in anguished amusement, given that this nano-chip would supposedly decrease crime. He shook his head, trying to clear his mind but the terrifying reality would not be denied. The Martian world he had known would soon come to an end. But was there a way out...?

He drove on and on through the Martian darkness and within a short time pulled up outside Orson' hut on the outskirts of the city. He checked his watch, it was 7.59pm. *'Good timing,'* he thought. Within minutes, Orson dashed over, opened the surface vehicle door and climbed in. He looked a little hesitant, his eyes reflecting his uncertainty.

"Okay Ivan, what's this all about? This is all a bit sudden."

"Not sure myself, to be honest, but here goes." He paused to find the right words.

"Well…"

"Without going into too much detail I met a lovely lady yesterday at the Philosophical Society."

"Okay… and?"

"We connected straight away… had an incredible conversation. Toward the end I mentioned the nano-chip and asked her thoughts on it. Like us she is dead against the idea. To cut a long story short she said that she has a friend that would love to meet me. He too opposes the new law. An unusual type is the impression she gave. In her own words… not the kind of person you meet every day."

"I see," said Orson, his voice low and strained. "So, what are you expecting from this person exactly? Orson eyed him sharply.

"I'm not sure." With that he drove away heading to the destination.

Both Ivan and Orson waited at the front door of a large hut in a remote area neither had really visited before. Martian wind circled about them, stirring up the dust which added to the sense of mystery they both felt. Orson nervously flapped at the dust on his coat while Ivan pressed the buzzer a second time. They were rewarded by the sound of footsteps and the door opened. It was Alicia.

"Ivan come in, and you too Sir. It's time... he's waiting." She smiled.

For a brief second it all seemed surreal to Ivan. He had met this lovely, intelligent, spiritual, angelic lady unexpectedly the day before at the Philosophical Society and now she was taking him and his friend to meet some unknown man who at this point remained nameless. He composed himself, simulating a calm he did not feel and stepped in, Orson following close behind. They followed as Alicia rapidly led the way down a long, wide cream-walled corridor until they reached a brightly lit room. There was a stairway...

Alicia turned around and said, "Bertrand is in his underground work chamber. You will understand why shortly."

She led them down the stairway ushering them into a large, brightly lit chamber, bolts and screws lying all around. Ivan's attention was immediately drawn to a large silver spherical machine. Then an old man with a full head of grey hair, suddenly came into view. He was dressed in a white robe.

"Time," he said abruptly. "This is the first time-machine ever built my friends. This time-sphere was designed with acute precision, a highly complex machine that defies the laws of science and time. Four years it took me to build, and I alone did it. This machine represents a thousand years of science and mathematics all rolled into one."

The man began walking over towards them with suave authority, his eyes beaming with confidence, bits of stubble poking from his chin. His geniality and wonderfully convoluted mind clearly displayed on his countenance.

"Can you imagine," he said, his voice now full of zeal. "This machine is capable of carrying a person not only into the past, but also into the future. But it is the past that interests me at present. To have found the key that unlocks the door of time is the greatest achievement within the sphere of science and technology. Not even our ancestors down on Earth managed to build such a machine. Now remember, the past, present and future are frozen in time and space. With this machine we can unlock that door and travel into the future but also move into the past."

Ivan stood there completely stunned and confused. He looked over at Alicia and Orson, then turned back to Bertrand and said, "Remarkable indeed sir, but I'm not sure what you are getting at."

The old man smiled and said, "It's time to test this mind-blowing theorem of space-time continuum. You my friend will travel back in time and kill the man who is currently responsible for bringing in the new law, the nano-chip. It's the only way to put an end to this evil... Thus, you will journey back in time and kill that man, the Supreme Leader, Roger J. Locke. He was the one that made the ultimate decision, the one to bring in the new law. And it was through him that the Governing Leaders formed and came into power. Thus, the solution is quite simple go back in time and kill him. Then you can return to natural time, a world where Roger J. Locke no longer exists. As a result, you will have hopefully wiped out the formation of this elite tyrant group... the Governing Leaders, restoring normality to the planet."

Ivan was stunned and would have laughed out loud but for the serious, adoring look Alicia gave the professor. Orson was also struggling to suppress his chuckles and Ivan gave him a sharp dig in the ribs with his elbow. Then the words of the wise robot Alexis, concerning quantum theory and retrocausality, which yesterday had seemed to make perfect sense, flooded his mind. Could the professor have truly built a time-machine? He began to believe. But Ivan was a human being and eventually he had to ask a very basic human question, "Why me...? If it's that simple, why wouldn't you go yourself?"

"The truth is... I'm an old, fragile man. I'm not in good health either. As for Alicia, well... she simply doesn't have the courage. A journey like this requires someone young, courageous, and strong. Perhaps your friend would be better suited for the task?"

Orson's eyes popped and he said, "What? No chance, there's no chance with me, so forget that."

"Then it's you Ivan. However, if you decline, I will have no choice. Are you willing to make the journey?"

Ivan hesitated. His forehead was sweaty. He was tense, caught in deep thought.

"What guarantees do I have that this machine works properly?"

"Well, the truth is it has never been tested, however I can assure you that in terms of its usage and function it's in first class working order. The overwhelming probability is that all will be well."

"So, I'm taking a minor risk then?"

"Don't allow your thalamic impulses to take control Ivan. Existence is a risk in itself. Remember, risk is the key factor in success. You need to change your mind-set. Think of it in these terms... In order to save humanity from this evil you will have to take a minor risk."

Ivan looked at Orson as he stood there silent and still, overwhelmed by what he was hearing, no longer finding any humour in the situation. It all felt beyond surreal. Then he looked at Alicia. She in turn looked at him in a way no one had ever looked at him before. She believed in the professor... in him.

Rubbing his forehead hesitantly, still not quite believing he was agreeing to this he said, "Okay Bertrand, I'll do it. I guess I will be classified a time-travelling murderer."

"Ivan you are doing this for the good of Mars. There is no time to ponder on metaphysical ethics. You take out one man to save the souls of millions of others."

Silence fell. Ivan's eyes strayed towards the time-machine. Thoughts surged through his mind. He said, "Bertrand, I'm not an expert in metaphysics but I do know that going back in time to kill this man could cause other changes, a ripple effect. This in turn could cause a fracture in time, creating another time-path. There will be inevitable changes throughout the course of time. My presence alone could alter history, the present, and in turn, the future. I could start a never-ending time shift. A chain reaction..."

"Yes Ivan. This is known as chaos theory. But given the severity of the situation I think it's worth the risk, regardless of the other variances. All that ultimately matters is that we try and rid Mars of this evil. We have no choice."

"Fine, however just because I kill Roger J. Locke, which in turn means that he no longer exists in our time, doesn't necessarily mean that we would have automatically wiped out the existence of the Governing Leaders. Perhaps someone else will bring them to power, then what? I could execute the job and come back and still find a planet dominated by these tyrants, headed by another Supreme leader."

"True, but that's the risk we must take. There are no absolute guarantees but what choice do we have? If you go back in time the probability is that you will return to a planet where there are no Governing Leaders imposing the nano-chip on the Citizens of Mars. Look at it like that."

Ivan's legs suddenly felt very wobbly.

"It seems to me Bertrand that the risks here are many, but yes, what choice do we have? If I don't try, we are all doomed anyway. I'll give it a shot and hope for the best. Shot being the operative word. So, where's the gun?"

Ivan half hoped there would not be one, delaying the inevitable but Bertrand walked over to a desk and from the draw pulled out a small silver ray-gun. He handed it to Ivan who placed it into his deep jacket pocket.

"Now, you will have to travel back 50 Martian years," said the Professor briskly. "Locke is now seventy. In other words, you are going to kill him when he's twenty. I've analysed this man's entire life, all his history. I have all the information and data necessary to accomplish the task. I have already input all that data into the time-machine. I have set the exact time, the exact date and exact location. You will balloon into existence directly outside his hut. Hopefully, you will remain unseen. Operating the machine is quite simple. Come, I will show you..."

Ivan hesitantly walked over to the spherical silver time-machine. The old man pressed a button which was fixed to its silver metallic frame.

"Now that's how you open the door, just press this button."

The time-machine hummed into life and started to drone as its door slid open, releasing a gush of vapour that instantly dissipated. Ivan bit his lips in apprehension. He could hear the noise of waking electronic components.

"Please take your seat," said Bertrand. "I will explain what you need to do."

Instantly both Alicia and Orson crowded over. Alicia hugged him tightly.

"I know it is risky Ivan, but this is the only way. Good luck."

She smiled warmly as he turned to kiss her soft cheek, a promise that their relationship would be further explored when he returned.

"Good luck my friend," said Orson shaking his hand, his voice suddenly tinged with fear. "You wanted a miracle solution. Well, I guess this is it. Who knows what will happen, the potential changes there will be, what the catastrophic ripple effect will be? But if it works then that will put an end to the Governing Leaders and the wicked new law and you my friend will be a hero."

Ivan had no reply to this. He turned and slid awkwardly into the seat. He watched the flashing lights on the control panel for a few seconds and then turned to look out. His eyes focused on Bertrand and he said, "When I return to this Martian reality will I return here, to this precise location and meet with you all again…?"

"Yes, but what is currently here may alter due to your journey. Hopefully, you will return here as it is now and meet with us again, but chaos theory dictates that there might be changes so be prepared."

Ivan pushed his feet into the glittering metal floor, wanting to feel something solid and tangible to anchor his swirling thoughts and feelings. Monitors flickered green and blue, bleeping and humming… a whole combination of computerized activity, highly sophisticated technology. Cold ventilated air began pouring in beneath him. Once in you couldn't see out. The spherical time-machine was completely sealed off with silver metal everywhere.

Bertrand's disembodied head suddenly appeared through the mist and calmly said, "Do you see that white lever, the one directly in front of you?"

"Yes, of course," replied Ivan.

"Well, all you need to do is push the lever forward, that's all. When you want to return, you do exactly the same. It's as simple as that. In terms of opening the door you just press that red button. See it?

"Yes."

"Are you ready?"

"Yes I am..."

"Okay, good luck Ivan. Mars' future lies in your hands."

As Bertrand pulled away, closing the door, he caught a last glimpse of Alicia and Orson watching solemnly in silent homage. Ivan drew breath, trying hard to compose himself. He could not quite believe what was happening. He never expected such an encounter, nor did he expect to ever be on such a dangerous mission, one which meant he had to go back in time to kill someone. He had never killed anybody in his life. *'Well Larson, you wished for a saviour, but I never thought it would be me,'* he thought and rubbing both hands nervously he pushed the white lever forward with his right arm. The bright lights abruptly faded into utter darkness. The time-machine started to shake and vibrate. All of time blazed...

A few minutes later the shaking and vibrating stopped. There was no sound at all. The lights reactivated. He was out of the darkness but where, when? He swallowed hard and pressed the red button. The door opened.

Cautiously, he stepped out planting his feet gratefully on the ground. The time-machine had just suddenly reappeared... a sudden mass of silver metal lying on the Martian soil. He had successfully travelled back in time... 50 Martian years... at least he hoped he had.

Ivan went to close the door, but then decided against it, just in case he had to get away quickly. He looked around in disbelief. No one was in sight. Luckily for him, the hut was located in a secluded zone. He focused on the building and slowly made his way towards it, pale Martian sunlight shining across the landscape, the sky blue. He pressed the buzzer twice not knowing what to expect exactly. What if Bertrand had miscalculated? What if Roger J. Locke wasn't there? What would he do? He heard footsteps. A well-dressed young man opened the door slowly.

"What can I do for you?" he said sharply.

Immediately Ivan knew it was him, the unmistakable voice and face a dead give-away. It was indeed the twenty-year-old Roger J. Locke. Although this was a younger version, Ivan could see the viciousness and arrogance embedded in his eyes and posture. In fact, they were more obvious now as the man had not had fifty years to learn how to hide it.

"Are you Roger J. Locke?" Ivan asked, just for absolute confirmation.

"Yes. Who might you be?"

Ivan coldly pulled out the ray-gun and fired. Everything moved in slow motion. The deadly beam of light seemed to travel at a slow dream-like pace... but within a fraction of a second, as if space, time, and matter, that raw material of the physical world had collapsed around them, liquefying and fading, both men were transported into darkness and subsequently, non-existence...

The lonely wind sighed and teased the dusty surface of the Red Planet. Mars was alone once again, quiet and still, endless miles of oxidised rock and gaping craters. Ivan Dobrovolski, Orson, the Philosophical Society and its incredible robots, Alicia, Bertrand had all ceased to exist with the firing of the ray-gun, physics granting them the grace of never knowing their culpability in creating a catastrophic ripple effect, so devastating that all Martian life, all of their reality had been wiped out in a flash.

The winds of Mars stroked the dunes gently. Mars bided... the ancient landscape quiescent, waiting for the children of the green blue celestial sphere known to its inhabitants as Earth to come and call it home.

Then...

Approximately forty minutes earlier they had been in orbit around the Red Planet. Then came the frightening journey down as they burnt their way through the thin Martian atmosphere. The descent vehicle shook violently. The ride was bumpy until they finally reached the ground and on touchdown the rocket thrusters ceased.

Commander Francis Jarre could hear nothing through the thick insulation of his pressure suit helmet except his own erratic breathing tinged with both excitement and fear. He believed he was one of the first men to actually land on Mars. In his reality he was.